MASSACRE

Longarm called ahead. He got no answer. He moved in out of line with the front door, got a blind corner between himself and anyone inside, and chased the muzzle of his Winchester over to flatten out against a 'dobe wall and inch his way to an open window.

He risked a quick peek, swore, and took a longer look into what seemed a Mexican verison of the last act of *Hamlet*.

As he counted the still forms sprawled across the tile floor inside, with the twilight from outside turning those pools of blood into puddles of jet-black ink, he made them to be four—a middle-aged man, a not-much-younger woman, an older woman, and a boy of about nine. He moved around to the rear door and worked his way forward through every room before he called Perrita in.

As she and her mule led his fresh palomino up to the hitching rail in the dooryard, Perrita asked if he'd found out why it was so dark inside.

To which Longarm could only reply, "I have . . ."

DON'T MISS THESE
ALL-ACTION WESTERN SERIES
FROM THE BERKLEY PUBLISHING GROUP

THE GUNSMITH by J. R. Roberts
Clint Adams was a legend among lawmen, outlaws, and ladies. They called him . . . the Gunsmith.

LONGARM by Tabor Evans
The popular long-running series about U.S. Deputy Marshal Long—his life, his loves, his fight for justice.

SLOCUM by Jake Logan
Today's longest-running action Western. John Slocum rides a deadly trail of hot blood and cold steel.

BUSHWHACKERS by B. J. Lanagan
An action-packed series by the creators of Longarm! The rousing adventures of the most brutal gang of cutthroats ever assembled—Quantrill's Raiders.

TABOR EVANS
LONGARM
AND THE
REDHEAD'S RANSOM

JOVE BOOKS, NEW YORK

LONGARM AND THE REDHEAD'S RANSOM

A Jove Book / published by arrangement with
the author

PRINTING HISTORY
Jove edition / January 2000

For information address: The Berkley Publishing Group,
a division of Penguin Putnam Inc.,
375 Hudson Street, New York, New York 10014.

The Penguin Putnam Inc. Wide Web site address is
http://www.penguinputnam.com

ISBN: 0-515-12734-5

A JOVE BOOK®
Jove Books are published by The Berkley Publishing Group,
a division of Penguin Putnam Inc.,
375 Hudson Street, New York, New York 10014.
JOVE and the "J" design
are trademarks belonging to Penguin Putnam Inc.

PRINTED IN THE UNITED STATES OF AMERICA

10 9 8 7 6 5 4 3 2 1

Chapter 1

There was no moon six hours after sundown and Los Apaches were said to be about. So the *posadero* and his people were afraid when they heard hoofbeats and rude shouts from the darkness out front. But a *posada* refusing entrance to strangers in the night is not a *posada* to show much profit. And so the three late arrivals on such a dark and windy night were greeted with cautious courtesy if not with open arms as they entered with a gust of raw wind from the east.

There were three of them. Two *vaqueros* of *la raza* and a woman in a dark Yanqui riding habit and veiled hat to go with her red hair and the few subdued words of English the *posadero*'s daughter heard from her as she took their order for *pulque* at a corner table. One of the men sat with the *gringa* in the corner as the other dickered with the *posadero* for a change of horses. This did not take long. The strangers were obviously in a hurry and offered many Yanqui dollars in addition to their three jaded mounts.

And then they were off, and as the *posadero* barred the door again, he was not unhappy to see the last of them, even though their short stay had been most profitable. He said so as he blew out the candles near the door. It was his daughter, clearing the small blue table in their corner, who said, *"Dios mio. La puta, esa mujer esta pendejada."*

Her father strode across the dimly lit interior to see what crazy thing the English-speaking whore had been up to and agreed, with an angry curse, when he saw how the silently seated woman had managed to vandalize the whitewashed adobe wall beside her chair.

She had used a nail or some other small sharp object to scratch a short message upside down in English. Nobody there understood enough to read what she had scrawled there. But Gordo, from the kitchen, was of the opinion that "HELP!" meant something like *Ayudame!* and they all agreed on what "POLICE!" had to mean. So the next day the *posadero* reported the unusual night visit to *los rurales* and, as luck and the depredations of Victorio's Apache raiders would have it, *los rurales* were on speaking terms with the Texas Rangers at the moment.

Hence in less than forty-eight hours, with the work week coming to a merciful close and a certain young widow up on Capitol Hill baking a peach pie for him, with an even sweeter dessert in mind, U.S. Deputy Marshal Custis Long got called back to the inner office of Marshal William Vail of the Denver District Court, who wasn't half as pretty.

The pudgy bullet-headed Billy Vail was only half visible in the blue haze of cigar smoke above his cluttered vest as the banjo clock on one oak-paneled wall warned his senior deputy it was time to get a leg on if he didn't want a mighty cold supper indeed. Grabbing the only chair on his side of the desk, Longarm, as he was better known around the Denver Federal Building, protested, "Can't this wait until a cold gray Monday morning, Boss? I just finished that infernal paperwork out front on my own time, and more civilized government offices close at noon of a purple-pissing Saturday!"

Billy Vail blew more smoke out both nostrils as he held up a sheaf of yellow Western Union paper, growling, "You'll have time to tell her you have to catch a night train for Texas if you run some. But if you don't make the southbound eight-fifteen, you can commend your soul to Jesus because your ass will belong to *me*, for this one's a hot potato direct from the White House!"

Lighting a sweeter-smelling three-for-a-nickel cheroot in self-defense and interested in spite of himself, Longarm dryly replied, "I purely hope it's not another invite to supper from the First Lady. Miss Lemonade Lucy Hayes ain't bad-looking, you understand, but you have to sip one of her mint juleps made without a whiff of liquor to really understand why I'd as soon sup somewhere else."

The married-up and now housebroken Billy Vail cocked a bushy brow at his somewhat younger and far better-looking senior deputy as he snorted, "My old woman is still after me about your scandalous suppers just down Sherman Street from our back fence. Nobody wants you to join them in Washington. I told you they wanted you to head for *Texas*. West Texas, Val Verde County officially. You know our State Department promised Mexico City our notorious El Brazo Largo would never invade Mexico again if they took back that declaration of war."

Longarm, as Brazo Largo was pronounced in English, shrugged and calmly observed, "I hadn't planned on going anywhere near Old Mexico this weekend, Boss. If I *had* been planning on another run south of the border, I can think of nicer parts to visit than you seem to be hinting at. As I recall those Burro Mountains south of, say, the railroad stop at Langtry, it ain't a friendly neighborhood at all. There's hardly anybody but mighty mean Mexicans or even meaner Indians holed up in such dry marginal range. Who down yonder might Miss Lemonade Lucy want us to invite back to the States, and for what?"

He'd spoken in jest. But Billy Vail replied, in a more serious way, "Her name would Fiona Palmer née Maguire, age twenty-two and by all accounts a looker with flaming red hair and a right fashionable hourglass figure. She was last seen headed into the Serrianas del Burro wearing a navy-blue riding habit and in the company of two men dressed as Mexican cowhands or bandits. The Rangers were sure they were bandits even before they read the ransom note that arrived by mail from Ciudad Acuña. That's where they figure she was kidnapped, Ciudad Acuña."

Longarm blew a thoughtful smoke ring and stared through it at his mental map of Estada Coahuila as he mused aloud, "That would be the last big border town upstream before that long stretch of nothing much along the Big Bend, right?"

Billy Vail, who'd ridden with the pre-war Texas Rangers in his own younger days, nodded curtly and said, "Damned right. Rough, tough town in rough wide-open spaces. Why in thunder she and her new husband, Little Dick Palmer of the Lazy P, chose such a place to honeymoon beats the liver and lights out of me and the Texas Rangers. But they did, and so there they were in the crowded *mercado mayor* in the cool of the evening when Little Dick Palmer turned around from admiring a clay pot, a straw hat, or whatever to discover that his bride was nowhere to be seen. He naturally asked, long and loud, only to get those soft smiles and shrugs of *Quien Sabe?* The Rangers figure—"

"I know how neighborhood crooks kidnap an Anglo gal in a Mexican market," Longarm said. "How come they call that husband of hers Little Dick, and has anybody considered *that* possible motive for a well-built bride to vanish on her honeymoon?"

Billy Vail snapped, "That ain't funny, and this is serious enough for a Cabinet meeting back East, dammit! Little Dick Palmer is around six feet tall, and the West Texas gals seemed to admire him a heap till he married up with the popular Fiona Maguire from Fort Stockton. He's the son and heir of *Big* Dick Palmer, owner of the Lazy P home spread and water rights, along with countless cows and about as many guns on his payroll as the U.S. Army has west of the Sabine. Big Dick Palmer is the reason they called that Cabinet meeting. Big Dick Palmer is an unreconstructed Rebel who rode under Hood as a Confederate colonel and still considers Robert E. Lee a big sissy for surrendering just as Texas was fixing to win. So even as we speak, Big Dick Palmer and his pissed-off offspring, the good-sized Little Dick, are gathering kith, kin, and anyone else who wants to ride with them for five dollars a day after the fucking Mexicans who made off with that ravishing and likely well-ravished redhead Miss Fiona."

Longarm whistled softly and decided, "A private posse of pissed-off Texicans riding into Mexico on their own? Aside from getting the poor gal killed for certain, they're likely to tangle with anyone from those Quill Indians riding with Victorio to the fair-sized Mexican army in the field along the border looking for Victorio or any other border jumpers!"

Vail sighed and said, "It gets worse. They don't call a Cabinet meeting every time some Texas riders tangle with *los federales*. It's understood that it's up to the Good Lord to look after village drunks, lunatics, and Texicans. I just told you the Rangers had traced Fiona Palmer west toward the Burro Mountains, and I mentioned the ransom note postmarked from Ciudad Acuña. What I left out was the ransom demanded by some son of a bitch calling himself El Pico."

Longarm said, "I've heard tell of El Pico. Some say he's a rebel fighting for the cause of Mejico Libre. Others say he's just another piss-pot *bandito* fighting for fun and profit in troubled times along the border."

Vail smiled knowingly and said, "That's why they've asked me to send you, unofficially, to see what can be done about that kidnapped redhead before all hell busts loose. Big Dick Palmer is rich as hell and appears ready to move Heaven and Earth to help his only son and a daughter-in-law he admires a heap. So a private invasion of Mexico is the least of Washington's worries. El Pico ain't asking for ransom in *cash*. He's demanded a ransom in *kind*. He says they'll rape and murder the poor gal unless somebody sends them six hundred Springfield .45 cavalry carbines and a hundred thousand rounds of .45-75 for the weapons."

Longarm whistled and decided, "Sounds like El Pico must be planning on expanding his band to a full regiment. But where's a private citizen supposed to get his hands on that much U.S. Army ordnance?"

Vail didn't hesitate to answer. "On the open market, of course. The War Department's been selling off army surplus cheap since the end of Reconstruction. And Army Ordnance canceled orders on the Springfield '73 carbine after its poor showing at the Little Bighorn. So that slow-but-sure breechloader, new or used, has become a glut on the market north of the border, and most anybody with the pocket jingle can buy long-range .45-75 rounds to fire from it, off more than half a dozen ammo factories."

Vail took a deep drag on his stogie, blew an octopus cloud of smoke across the desk at Longarm, and added, "Mexico City is more worried about the Palmers running guns to Mexican rebels than they are about more armed and dangerous riders in the Burro Mountains. So Washington has warned Big Dick Palmer not to ransom his daughter-in-law with guns or ammo, and promised in return to rescue her instead. That's where you come in."

Longarm gasped incredulously and demanded, "Why me? Have the U.S. Army and Texas Rangers both gone out of business this summer?"

Vail said, "They have as far as Fiona Palmer is concerned. In a rare display of common sense the Mexican and American armies have been working together along the border on Victorio and his Bronco Apache raiders. Even if our cavalry had the men to spare, the Mexicans would resent a criminal investigation south of their border, and even if the Mexicans *didn't* care, as you just pointed out, such wild bullshit figures to get that redhead killed before they ever cut her kidnappers' trail."

Before Longarm could ask, Billy Vail said, "The Rangers might or might not have a better chance down Mexico way if Washington allowed Texas that much free rein. But President Hayes caught enough hell for ending Reconstruction and allowing Texas to replace those carpetbagging State Police with Ranger companies who'd fought on the losing side against the Union. So he's not about to cut the Texas Rangers in on these delicate matters."

"What about *los rurales* or even *los federales*?" Longarm asked in a wistful tone as he found himself longing for more peach pie than anyone might manage before that southbound eight-fifteen.

Vail shrugged and said, "If either the Mexican rangers or Mexican army had the least notion where El Pico's hideout might be, they'd have likely brought the gal back dead or alive by this time. The town law was no help to Little Dick Palmer when he reported his bride to be missing in Ciudad Acuña. But it was *los rurales* who cut the sign she'd left by scratching a plea for help on a wall when her kidnappers weren't looking. She never got to finish, but did get to sign her name, and part of her message said she'd overheard the kidnappers saying they were taking her to a place called Escondrijo Yaqui in the Burro Mountains."

Longarm frowned thoughtfully and asked if the missing gal spoke Spanish. When Billy Vail allowed that beat the shit out of him, Longarm explained, "If she don't, that explains why she'd leave a message in English for Mexican lawmen. A destination called Escondrijo Yaqui only works if they were shitting her deliberately in English."

Billy Vail savvied enough Border Mexican to do his own rough translating. So he decided, "I'll allow you shouldn't find many Yaqui east of the Big Bend if you'll allow me to point out you won't find all that many Sioux in Sioux City or Cheyenne in that Wyoming railroad town. Real Yaqui in a real Yaqui hideout in *any* fool mountains would never allow Mexicans of any description to hide out with 'em. Yaqui are as cross-grained towards outsiders as any Indians I can think of. So you might be right about them fibbing to their captive. Or there might be some canyon, cave, or whatever in the Burros known to the local folks as an old Yaqui hideout. You'll know better once you scout around down yonder, won't you?"

Longarm cocked a brow and murmured, "I reckon. Let me get this straight. You want this child to ford the Rio Bravo somewhere near the Burro Mountains and just sneak about in thinly settled semi-desert in high summer, looking for a gal I've never seen in the company of Mexican outlaws I don't know, who might be somewhere near a place I doubt I'll find on any fucking map?"

Vail sounded cheerful, considering, when he replied, "We know it's not on any map. We looked. I'm not the one who wants you to go anywhere in Old Mexico. If it was up to *me* you'd stay the hell north of the border, as you've often heard me order you to. But what can I tell you? I just work here. Somebody at headquarters we owe a lot to must have heard about some of your earlier visits down Mexico way. I told you how Mexico City pissed and moaned about you and your Mexican rebel pals wiping out that army column over in the Baja, and they were even *more* pissed off when you stole that Mexican gunboat on another such occasion. So, knowing you by name, whether Mexico could ever prove the charges or not, somebody in Washington decided you were just the one to send on such a delicate mission—unofficially, that is. As far as anyone but you, me, the lampost, and a handful higher up will ever hear, I've sent you back East to attend a conference on modern law enforcement methods. Your name will appear on the register of a Washington hotel, should anyone ever get around to checking up on your official reasons for not being on duty here in Colorado, see?"

Searching in vain for an ashtray, Longarm flicked his cheroot above the threadbare carpet as he replied, "I don't see why anybody higher than Cabinet rank would be checking up on us. I take it Mexico City has approved this delicate situation, in spite of past misunderstandings betwixt me and that total cocksucker El Presidente Diaz?"

Billy Vail shook his head and morosely replied, "Not exactly. Those in Washington who really know the two-faced tyrant share your opinion of him. But Wall Street and all too many American newspapers admire Diaz for establishing a long-overdue stable government in Mexico."

Longarm snorted, "That's what Wall Street calls a government that makes everybody wallow in horse shit, a stable government."

Vail pointed out, "Everybody but a few vested interests and the stockholders in many a U.S. mining or trading firm. Do you want to argue Mexican politics, or would you like to talk about your mission to Mexico, my idealistic youth?"

Longarm snorted, "I got the unofficial picture. You want me to jump the border unofficially and see if my unofficial Mex pals can tell me how I can get that redhead back without arming a whole regiment of Mexicans I don't know shit about. I get along with decent Mexicans. I even know some *rurales* well enough to drink with unofficially. But what if I run into *official rurales*, packing those reward papers on the head of El Brazo Largo?"

"You'll be in a whole lot of trouble unless you can talk or fight your way out," said Billy Vail flatly.

His senior deputy was a good poker player. So Billy Vail stared at Longarm for a spell before he added in a more fatherly tone, "Nobody has the power to order anything that wild directly, if you consider this mission too big a boo, old son."

Longarm rose to his considerable height and adjusted the hang of the .44-40 riding cross-draw under his tobacco-tweed frock coat as he said, "I got more important things to jaw about before that eight-fifteen pulls out. So order me no more orders and I'll tell you fewer lies when and if I ever get back."

Vail looked away and murmured, "See that you get back then. I'll never speak to you again if those outlaws or *los rurales* kill you."

Chapter 2

The home spread of the Lazy P holdings occupied high ground half a day's ride up the brushy floodplain of the Devil River. Nobody with a lick of sense built closer to a seasonable stream in such a contrary climate. Big Dick Palmer's daddy had come by the earlier Spanish land grant of the apparently extinct Fuentes family by vaguely sinister means the Palmers never talked about. So the sprawling complex of 'dobe walls, red-tile roofs, and whitewashed pole corrals was shaded by fair-sized ash and pecan trees.

Longarm was glad as he rode in aboard the livery nag he'd hired for him and his personal McClellan saddle near the railroad stop at Del Rio. The day had dawned hot, and hadn't cooled worth mentioning by the time he rode in near siesta time in a field outfit the current reform Administration might have frowned upon. For a man who rode out under a West Texas sun in high summer wearing the approved suit and vest of a U.S. deputy marshal on duty was a man who'd always wanted to experience heatstroke.

Longarm had naturally left his Winchester '73 in its saddle boot, and never drew the double-action Colt .44-40 riding cross-draw on his left hip unless he had to. So he found it right unfriendly when half a dozen gunhands rode out to meet him half a mile from their tree-shaded home spread to the west.

Longarm reined in to just sit his jaded livery nag in his own sweaty-crotched jeans and sticky denim work shirt as the Lazy P hand in the lead called out, "If you're the sawbones they sent for, you're late as well as mighty informal-looking. If you're out here about the other business you may have heard of, we'll coffee and cake you but the deal is off for now."

Longarm called back, "I'm neither a doctor nor a gun for hire. I'm the law. Federal. I know your boss has pulled in his horns for the time being. Who's sick?"

The point rider, a burlier Anglo who looked a tad older but not any shorter than the tall, tanned Longarm, replied, "The boss. Big Dick has come down with a ferocious bellyache. Miss Aurora fears it might be a mortified appendix such as Brigham Young just died from. So when they called down that someone was riding in . . ."

"I follow your drift," Longarm said. "Any sawbones driving up from Del Rio ought to be anxious as me to get out of this infernal sun. So I'll just take you up on that coffee and cake unless you and your boys would rather sunbathe out here with me."

The point rider laughed, said they called him Laguna Jacobs, and led the way back to the big house, where they were greeted as they dismounted by a handsome woman standing on the veranda in a lavender print summer frock that complimented her silver hair considerably.

Anyone could see her hair had gone gray prematurely, although she was likely ten years older than Longarm. Laguna introduced him to their boss's wife, Miss Aurora Palmer. As some Mexican kids took charge of the ponies out front, Longarm followed the lady of the house and her ramrod inside. He didn't ask how come the other riders never followed. No ranch hands lower in rank than their foreman rated coffee and cake in the big house on any Anglo spread in West Texas. English-speaking Texas had been mostly settled by Scotch-Irish from the Old South, and while they'd perforce adopted some new ways west of, say, Longitude 100, sitting down to table with the servants wasn't one of them.

But Miss Aurora never acted snooty as she held court at the foot of a linen-covered table set up under a grape arbor out back. They were joined soon after they'd started by Little Dick Palmer, all six feet four of him, wearing fresh-laundered jeans and a fresh cotton shirt Longarm could only envy, since the fluttering grape leaves above them could only do so much about the noonday sun.

They were served iced sangria punch as well as coffee with their cake by a pretty little *mestiza* in fandango skirts and an off-the-shoulder pleated blouse of homespun cotton. Their older hostess must have noticed how the younger gal flustered when Longarm thanked her in Spanish. Aurora tried to sound smoother than she likely felt when she introduced Little Dick as her stepson and coyly added she felt more like a big sister to the twenty-five-to-thirty-year-old cuss.

Little Dick wasn't trying to sound smooth as he flatly asked Longarm why he was this far north of the border when those fucking greasers were holding his poor bride somewhere south of the same.

Aurora gasped, "Dickie, please remember your manners!"

Longarm said soothingly, "I might cuss in mixed company, ma'am, if it was my own bride I'd had stolen from me on our honeymoon."

Turning to the bitter-lipped Little Dick, Longarm explained he'd ridden up from the border before crossing it because he'd found it best to start at one end of a trail and then follow it from there.

Little Dick growled, "This ain't where I lost my Fiona. You can ask anyone in these parts if we didn't get hitched over in Comstock, spend just one night here, and drive down for our honeymoon in Old Mexico."

Longarm nodded, but said, "That was one of the things I was wondering about. I was wondering how come a well-fixed Anglo couple wanted to honeymoon in a dinky border town such as Ciudad Acuña. What was the big attraction down Mexico way?"

"Mexico," replied Little Dick with no hesitation before he went on to explain. "Fiona was an army brat who'd never been to Old Mexico. I *told* her we could come by the same straw *vaqueros* and hot tamales in San Antone, where the hotel linen smells cleaner. But she allowed she'd never been out of the U.S. of A. in spite of all the army posts she'd lived on with her own folks."

"Fiona's father is, or was, a sergeant major," the lady of the house declared. "He was just getting set to retire when Dickie met her in Fort Stockton. We have a beef contract with the War Department, you see."

Little Dick Palmer turned to her. "This lawman ain't interested in where my Fiona might have come from, Aurora. They sent him to find out where Fiona *went* with them fucking greasers, see?"

Aurora Palmer rose from the table, calm-faced but red as a beet, to flounce out of sight through one of the doorways opening onto the back veranda as Little Dick muttered, "Good. Now mayhaps we can talk. Don't you have some other chores to tend to Laguna?"

The foreman's face was sort of flushed too as he allowed he sure did and excused himself from the table. As soon as they were alone, the blunt-spoken Little Dick nodded at Longarm and said, "This is between you and me. I didn't want to say it in front of anyone else, but my Fiona just couldn't get enough of my cock and she said so. I fucked her in the morning, during La Siesta, and every fucking night, out here and down in Ciudad Acuña, all three ways. She loved me true and took it from me up her ass and down her throat whenever I asked her to. But she did it all *willing*. I never did nothing to that pretty little thing she didn't *want* me to a *lot*!"

Longarm sipped some sangria as he chose his words. Then he calmly asked, "We heard the two of you were married up. It never crossed my mind that a honeymooning couple wouldn't be acting natural in private. Why did you feel I needed to hear such intimate details?"

Little Dick said, "You're going to hear how some suspect Fiona left me willing. It ain't true that Irish Catholic women are more suited to *hombres* of their own faith. Fiona assured me dog-style that my Protestant pecker suited her just fine, and it ain't true she wanted to visit Old Mexico in hopes of meeting up with some sneaky Latin lover!"

Longarm didn't answer as he polished off the last of his cake. So Little Dick demanded, "Answer me this if she run off with some damn Mex. Why would any gal running off with another man scribble a cry for help on any damn wall if she *liked* him so much? I'm dead certain Fiona was kidnapped, no matter what anyone may say!"

Longarm quietly asked, "Who's been intimating she could have run off with another man of her own free will? Your stepmother?"

Little Dick blinked in surprise and asked who'd told him.

Longarm said, "Lucky guess. You told me Miss Fiona was neither Texas-bred nor a member of your family's faith. How did you manage that at the wedding over in Comstock, by the way?"

"Methodist minister said he was willing if Fiona was willing. Fiona was born Irish Catholic without anyone consulting her in advance, and Dame Fortune dealt me a Protestant hand without asking. But neither of us were religious enough to argue about the small print in books neither of us read all that regular. Fiona said she'd been with this other army brat to a Hebrew service one time and didn't see what all the fuss was about."

Longarm nodded soberly and replied, "You have to attend, say, an old-time Cheyenne sun dance before the rites of different religions seem all that unusual to a neighborly eye. Your Miss Fiona sounds like an agreeable young lady with a natural curiosity about Old Mexico, and gals who run off with other men hardly ever send ransom notes home to the husband they've deserted."

The husband of the missing redhead said, "Damned right. I've asked our Mex help what they've heard about this fucking El Pico, and they say he's an ugly old ogre who weighs three hundred pounds and stands nigh seven feet tall in his fancy-stitched boots. They call him a 'peak' because he's so big, and Fiona said my cock was more than big enough for her. So why would she run off with a giant greaser?"

Before Longarm had to answer that, the little *mestiza* serving wench came back out on the veranda to shyly tell them they were wanted by Don Ricardo Grande inside. So they followed her through the depths of the nearly windowless adobe sprawl to a master bedroom, where Big Dick Palmer lay propped up atop the bedclothes in a flannel nightgown with a Navajo blanket over his legs, looking pale and goosefleshed in spite of the heat. His hair and mustache were going gray, but not as gray as the hair of his much younger second wife, or maybe more than second, who was seated on the far side of the bed with some broth she couldn't get him to take.

Aurora Palmer looked up wearily and said, "I told him we had a visitor from the Justice Department. He needs that damned doctor way more, but he insisted on seeing you, Deputy Long."

Longarm dropped to one knee on his side of the bed to gently ask the obviously mighty sick cattle baron what he might do for him.

Big Dick Palmer rolled his oyster-gray eyes like a stuck pig and moaned, "I ain't got time for this delicate shit. Lord only knows how much time I have left. For I've never felt this bad before, and I took a .52-caliber Yankee ball in the shin at Chickamauga."

"Where might you be hurting right now?" asked Longarm, adding in a soothing tone, "That doc from Del Rio ought to be here most anytime."

Big Dick Palmer moaned, "All over. But mostly in my guts. Feels like I need to burp, or fart, or both. I'm sorry, wife, but you heard the man ask, and take that infernal soup away from me. Just smelling it makes me want to puke, only I can't seem to puke neither."

Aurora got up to leave the room with the broth. The poor gal seemed to leave the room a lot when the Palmers, father or son, talked sort of country in front of her.

Big Dick told Longarm, "I want you to know before she comes back. I'm dying. Don't ask me how I know. I don't know what the fuck might be *wrong* with me. But nobody could feel this awful and *live*. So about that ransom El Pico is demanding . . ."

"We can't let him have half the guns and ammunition he's asking for," Longarm explained. "I ain't supposed to tell you this. But the U.S. Tenth Cav just got orders to intercept any arms shipped out this way *before* they can be mule-packed anywhere near the border."

Big Dick and his good-sized son and heir exchanged glances before Big Dick snorted, "There ain't no U.S. Tenth Cav. The Yankees put six hundred niggers on horseback and told 'em they were cavalry troopers! Is that what you call a cavalry regiment, by the Great Horned Spoon?"

Life was too short to argue with women or unreconstructed Rebels. So Longarm said, "By any name a rose would smell the same, and Uncle Sam ain't going to allow all that ordnance to fall into the hands of Mexican bandits. You have my word El Pico is no more than a big shit. You see, I have friends down Mexico way who've assured me many a so-called rebel can act worse than the total bastards riding for their so-called government."

He saw the sick cattle baron was getting more upset. As that little serving wench came in with some cold wet towels on a tray, Longarm told the older man, "My own friends south of the border can likely show me the way to El Pico without my having to arrive bearing gifts. Some of the Mex pals I can call on for help can be mean as hell in their own right. So I might be able to get your daughter-in-law back without El Pico carrying out his threats against her, if she's still alive."

Little Dick, looming behind Longarm, gasped, "Don't say that! Fiona *has* to still be alive! What good would she be to those outlaws if they killed her?"

Longarm didn't answer. If they couldn't see you could demand ransom for a dead gal as easily as you could an unwilling guest who scratched messages on walls, there'd be no kindness in pointing out that if the authorities on both sides of the border knew about that message left on *posada* plaster, the kidnappers she'd been writing about likely also knew what she'd done by this time.

As the pretty *mestiza* soothed Big Dick's brow with a cool compress, the older but still pretty Aurora Palmer returned with a paunchy cuss packing a doctor's bag. Longarm didn't argue when the lady of the house took the towels away from the *mestiza* and told her to show Longarm to a guest room. He agreed it might make more sense to talk about their missing daughter-in-law later on, before he rode back to Del Rio in the cooler shades of evening.

He followed the pretty little Mexican along a dark corridor smelling of candle wax and castile soap to a heavy oak door she unlocked for him. As he moved into the dimly lit chamber, cooled a mite by its thick 'dobe walls being rooted in Mother Earth, he saw they'd brought his McClellan, saddlebags, and Winchester in and draped them over the oak footboard of the bedstead.

The pretty little *mestiza* slammed the door shut and threw the heavy wrought-iron barrel bolt to lock it as she told him in Spanish they might be safer if anyone passing by assumed they were only in there *"hacer el amor."*

Longarm had to allow she was putting on a mighty convincing act as she calmly suited actions to her words by shucking her pleated blouse to reveal a brace of turgid nipples aimed his way from tits the size and apparent firmness of two melon halves. But when she unwound the sash of her skirts, she sounded more worried than wanton as she soberly assured him, "You could be in great danger here, El Brazo Largo!"

Chapter 3

Longarm removed his hat while the pretty little thing took to acting even more peculiar. She'd moved her tawny naked form over to the bed stead and sat down demurely on the covers to creak the bedstead with her shapely bare ass while loudly moaning, "*Estoy embrujada! Te adoro! Tienes mi corazón en tus manos.*" Meanwhile, Longarm held his own breath with one ear pressed to the door.

A million years crept by. Then, sure enough, he heard a soft dirty snicker, followed by the sounds of retreating footsteps on the tiles outside. So he moved over by the bedstead to drop his Stetson over the hornless pommel of his army saddle as he softly asked, "Who might that have been out yonder just now?"

The naked little *mestiza* lay back across the covers to spread her solid brown thighs invitingly as she husked, "*Quien sabe?* Many are most curious about El Brazo Largo and we were told you might be down our way again. They might come back. You had better take off all your clothes and help me see if I can sound more convincing."

Longarm felt no call to fuss with a naked lady in such a position. So he draped his gunbelt over a bedpost, and sat down beside her to shuck his boots as he politely asked how she might be called and who'd told her he might be some gent called El Brazo Largo.

She said, "*Me llamo Juanita, pero* my friends just call me Nita. El Brazo Largo is known to those of us who follow La Causa de Libertad as a tall handsome Anglo *mariscal segundo* with many connections to our *compañeros* south of the Rio Bravo. When I heard you say as much to Don Ricardo and his son, was not *dificil* for to guess who you had to be. *Pero* for why are you taking so long for to get undressed? Do you find me *repugnant* or is it my mixed blood you find so *repulsivo?*"

Longarm just hated to see a woman cry. So before Nita could, he took her in his bare arms with his socks left on, and assured her of his greatest respect while he rolled her on her back and mounted her missionary-style as she kissed him in French.

Then a grand time was had by all and if anyone was listening out in the hall, it served them right for not getting together with pals of their own during La Siesta.

Folks new to the sunny dry climates that Hispanic folks preferred to settle in learned to plan ahead for the three-or-four-hour siesta during the hottest hours of the day. There were no rules saying you had to spend your siestas catching up on your resting, reading, making love, or jerking off. You could tend to your stamp collection or build a boat in a bottle during your siesta, as long as you were holed up somewhere cool and shady while it was downright dangerous to be out and about. So most folks spending high summer in Siesta Country liked to plan ahead for such private times, unless they were just drunks or natural sleepyheads.

Knowing this, Longarm pounded Nita to glory and shot his own wad in her, before he suddenly rolled off and rose sweaty and still hard to draw his six-gun from its holster on the bedpost and whisper to her, "Hold my place. I'll be right back. But don't let on I'm anywhere else, *querida mia*!"

So the hot and bothered Nita, bless her little *corazón*, went on moaning and groaning words of passion as she bounced on the bedstead so Longarm could pad to the door in his socks, silently throw the bolt, and follow the muzzle of his cocked .44-40 out into the dimly lit hallway.

It was just as well for all concerned there was nobody there. He'd have felt silly explaining gunplay in his birthday suit with a raging erection. So he ducked back inside, shut the door, bolted it, and rejoined Nita on the bedstead to holster his six-gun and his raging erection at the same time.

It was easy. Nita had rolled over on her hands and knees to present her unquenched ring-dang-doo dog-style at about the same level as the holster hanging from the nearby bedpost.

Longarm gripped a softly padded hipbone with either hand, and as most old bed partners knew, dog-style was about the best position for enjoying casual conversation and calm coitus at the same time. So as they took their own sweet time, Longarm was able to question her as much as he felt Billy Vail might want him to.

He learned from the gal who worked there as a taken-for-granted maid-of-all-work that both Big and Little Dick Palmer had seemed to think more of the missing redhead than Miss Aurora had. Nita assured him he'd never heard the two gals really fighting, but she'd heard each insult the other when the other had been out of the room. The younger Fiona, more popular with the Mexican help, had implied that her stepmother-in-law seemed more popular with some of the Anglo help than a respectable woman with an ailing husband might have acted. As Nita arched her spine to take him deeper, she explained how Miss Aurora had sniffed at the Papist ways of her Irish-Catholic stepdaughter-in-law. That was what Miss Aurora had called rosary beads on a dresser and a *crucifijo* on the wall, Papist ways. Longarm knew better than to ask how much such *simpatico* notions had had to do with Miss Fiona getting on so much better with the Spanish-speaking folks on the Lazy P. He'd learned by keeping his mind open and his mouth shut that men and women of good will, on both sides, could misunderstand the shit out of one another's natural ways. He'd had Protestants assure him Catholics were idol worshippers, Catholics tell him those poor doomed Protestants didn't believe in Jesus, while both agreed the Mormons out Utah way sacrificed virgins to their pagan gods, the Smith brothers. So he asked Nita to tell him more about her suspicions concerning Miss Aurora's less religious activities.

Nita allowed she had to come first. So he made her, came in her as well, and got a smoke going for the two of them as the *mestiza* filled him in on the more personal habits of the household where she'd been working unobtrusively.

Nita said she'd once caught Miss Aurora and Laguna Jacobs, the ramrod, alone in the pantry in the dark. Nita had been carrying a lighted candle as she'd gone in there for some squeezing lemons for poor old Don Ricardo Grande. So she had to agree with Longarm that lots of folks wound up in the dark around sundown when there didn't seem to be a lamp or candlestick handy.

He said, "It ain't as if you can just wave your hand and light all the lamps in the house at once, you know. What were the two of them doing in there, and how come Laguna Jacobs has a Mexican nickname if he's so all-fired Anglo?"

Nita passed the cheroot back and commenced to toy with the moist hairs on Longarm's belly as she thought back and decided, "They were only talking, as far as I could see. They were both fully dressed and standing against opposite walls. But was a small room and they could have moved apart *muy pronto* as I opened the door."

Longarm repeated his question about "Laguna."

Nita explained the other Anglo riders had hung it on their boss a spell back. He'd not only taken up with a *muchacha india* from Chihuahua, but they'd caught him sharing Indian grub sent to her from back home, where her people were called Lagunas because they spent so much time around the salt ponds or lagoons of their desert basin.

Like their distant Paiute cousins around the more famous Great Salt Lake of Utah Territory, the somewhat primitive Laguna Indians of Northern Mexico were notorious for the "fish cakes" they whipped up from saltwater, brine-shrimp, buffalo-gnat larva, and slimy green pond scum to bake in the sun like mud pies before serving them for supper or sending them by mail to homesick Lagunas in other parts.

Longarm had always been ready to try anything once. So he'd tried a Laguna fish cake, *once*. He agreed with Nita that a white man would really have to admire a gal to share such shit with her regularly. When he asked Nita whether Laguna Jacobs spoke Nahuatl, as most Mexicans called Ho Hada or Uto-Aztec, she allowed Jacobs could get by in both Spanish and Nahuatl if he had to. Nita commenced to toy with Longarm's limp organ-grinder as she asked what difference it made whether another couple jawed in one lingo or another while they shared such private moments.

Longarm explained, "My boss calls what I'm up to the process of eliminating. I won't be able to ask such questions once I leave here."

She began to stroke him as she asked what he suspected Laguna Jacobs of. She said, "I do not care for him. He thinks he is so big, and one time he made a rude remark about my *chupas*. But I do not think he had anything to do with the abduction of La Señorita Fiona. To begin with, he was here on El Rancho when she vanished south of the Rio Bravo. For another *she* too was on what you could call most friendly terms with Señor Jacobs."

Longarm set the cheroot aside as he muttered, "That just goes to show you you can't tell a lady's man by his cover. You say the ladies of the house might be fooling with the hired help. What about the *men* of the house, Big or Little Dick?"

Nita commenced to fiddle with his belly hairs some more as she grudgingly allowed that neither the ailing boss nor his good-looking son and heir had ever remarked on her *chupas*. She'd been told that the older Don Ricardo had been raised strictly by a momma who'd felt that the slaves she'd brought west with her and the Mexican hired help had to be kept in their places, and by the time she'd died, the older Don Ricardo had married up with the Doña Lucinda everyone still respected—and a stiff-necked former Confederate colonel had wept openly over.

She declared, "Don Ricardo Grande is still *muy hombre,* or he was until this *enfermedad* came over him. Now he will not even eat. *Pero* some of the *vaqueros* say he used to ride into Comstock for to visit a certain *casa de idolatria* before he wed La Señora Aurora the year before last."

Longarm frowned thoughtfully, moved Nita's sneaky little hand from where she'd just snuck it, and asked her to tell him more about the no-longer-young but recently married-up Miss Aurora, explaining how a woman who'd likely been married at least once before might have a roving eye to go with a sickly second or third husband.

But Nita said neither she nor any of the other help knew anything about Aurora Palmer's past. So he steered the gossip towards Little Dick Palmer, and there the gal who worked under him was on much firmer ground. It appeared Little Dick, despite his size and build, had been raised as a sort of sissy by his real momma, the late respected Lucinda. La Doña Lucinda had had her boy all to herself during the four years the man of the house had been off to the war back East. So Little Dick had learned to read from the Good Book and her Methodist hymnals. The open-minded Longarm had to allow Methodists were a tad more easygoing than some Protestant sects based on the preachings of John Calvin, but Southern Methodist preachers of the Old South had been hell on slap-and-tickle in the servants' quarters, or come to study on it, most anywhere else.

Nita said nobody working there could say whether the younger Palmer had been a natural man or the virgin some suspected when he'd married up with that missing redhead.

But from the way they'd carried on the one night they'd spent on the home spread after their wedding over in Comstock, he'd sure enjoyed *la cosita* once he had one of his own to mess with. When she calmly added that more than one *mujer* on the payroll was looking forward to consoling Don Ricardo Poco for his loss, the lawman she was groping suspected he savvied why she'd been so anxious to share this siesta with *him.*

He'd learned as a red-faced boy back in West-by-God-Virginia that gals could brag as much about their conquests as men, whether they'd really gotten any or not, and since then he'd learned that Mexican gals could brag even more boldly, not having old John Calvin looking sternly down on them, and figuring that a celibate priest might not know what they were giggling about behind their fans. So, as the notorious El Brazo Largo, he owed a lot to some of those rebel gals he'd danced the fandango with on earlier occasions down this way. The man who'd said it paid to advertise had likely treated a few barefoot Mexican gals with the mixture of barnyard rutting and common courtesy that seemed to make them feel they'd met up with the one and original Don Juan. Longarm had read somewhere how the famous Casanova had confided that the simple use of soap and water, combined with asking politely, had been the secret of his success in an era of powdered wigs and cruder manners towards the weaker sex.

So seeing she was surely going to brag on all this to the other *mujeres* on the Lazy P, and seeing it paid to advertise, Longarm let Nita have her wicked way with his old organ-grinder, figuring she'd deserve some more of it if she could get it up again, sticky as it was getting, with the afternoon sun beating down on however thick a roof of terra-cotta tiles over a layer of tamped earth laid on heavy planking. What she was doing sure felt good. But his belly hairs were more than damp now, and Nita was sweating considerably as she skillfully beat his meat for him.

He decided, "We'd better save some for later, after we catch some sleep and things cool off towards sundown. Do you know whether there might be some socks or underdrawers that kidnapped redhead might have left in a laundry hamper nobody's emptied as yet?"

The gal found the question so surprising she let go of him to ask what in thunder he wanted with a missing redhead's dirty drawers.

He explained, "They might come in handy later if I can beg, borrow, or steal some bloodhounds. You folks call 'em *perros sabuesos*. Mind you don't go handing me such unmentionables in mixed company, should you find any I can use. Slip 'em in one of those saddlebags at the foot of this bed when nobody else is in here."

She allowed she would. So he asked her why she'd told him earlier that he was in danger in those parts.

She told him she'd meant he shouldn't head back down into Old Mexico in such trying times. She said the border was being heavily patrolled because of Victorio's reservation jump to the north, and when Longarm said he'd already considered that, Nita said, "Then consider that *los rurales* have added to their standing offer for the head of El Brazo Largo and this time they know he is coming!"

He asked her how she knew that.

Nita shrugged her sweaty bare shoulders and morosely replied, "If I and the other *pobrecitos* working this far north of the Rio Bravo were expecting another visit from El Brazo Largo, do you not think at least one *denunciador chingado* must have told *los rurales* your own government is sending you on a fool's mission right into their own waiting hands?"

Chapter 4

Everyone out there but Big Dick Palmer seemed to feel friskier late that afternoon. A servant had been sent to roam the halls with supper chimes by the time Nita had ducked out to return a few minutes later wearing fresh duds and an innocent smile for the benefit of the two Mexican boys hauling hot and cold bathwater to Longarm's room for him.

Nita told him the lady of the house had invited him to spend the night. Longarm waited until he'd joined Miss Aurora, Little Dick, Laguna Jacobs, and that same old paunchy but sickly-looking sawbones from town, Doc Morrison. Everybody got to sit around a low-slung coffee table, sipping sangria or bourbon and branch water, while the hired help and a grandfather clock against a far wall decided when it was time to serve supper. That gave Longarm plenty of time to explain he wanted to ride down to Ciudad Acuña after sundown and see if he couldn't make it before that central market closed for the night. You didn't need to explain how late Mexican markets stayed open to West Texas folks. Eastern bluestockings tended to turn up their noses at the hours kept out in Spanish-speaking parts of the West, not understanding how both Mexican and Anglo followers of the siesta custom made up for the lost hours in the middle of the day by staying open for business way past closing times or even bedtimes in, say, Boston. Pretty little Nita, toting in fresh ice for their drinks with a Mona Lisa smile, was the only one with just cause to comment on his crossing the border unofficially in the dark. Or so he sure hoped.

Little Dick allowed that in that case he'd be proud to ride down yonder with Longarm to show him around the scene of the crime. He added, "I can't wait to introduce you to the sweet old lady selling candied cockroaches two yards away who smiles with no teeth as she assures you or any other lawman she remembers *me,* examining riding quirts one stand over, but can't recall any Anglo redhead in a bright green summer frock, for Gawd's sake."

Laguna Jacobs piped up. "I'll ride with you, Boss. That way you won't have to ride home alone and if push comes to shove, I know my way around down yonder. I talk a couple of Indian lingos as well as fair Spanish, and a lot of them old country women selling stuff nobody in old Spain would consider eating don't speak as much Spanish as *me*."

But Aurora Palmer shook her silvery head and pointed out, "That would leave me here alone to cope with this emergency, and you know I can barely speak Spanish, Mr. Jacobs."

So Longarm never asked whether Laguna spoke Nadéné, or Apache, as well as the Nahuatl that Chihuahuas, Comanches, Lagunas, Yaquis, and such could follow. He asked how his unseen host, Big Dick, was doing.

The lady of the house told him to ask the doctor. Doc Morrison said, "Mighty poorly and sort of mysterious. My first thought was that he'd come down with stomach ulcers from all this worry. He's been vomiting half the fluids we've been able to get down him and showing traces of blood in his otherwise watery vomit. He tells me he had the trots a day or so before he commenced to feel really poorly, with the cold sweats and a burning feeling I just can't pick up with any thermometer. He *says* he feels *cold,* in spite of this hot spell we've been having, and Herr Gabriel Fahrenheit backs his complaints. Cold sweats with burning innards and gooseflesh on the outside are a new one on this old country doctor."

Longarm stared thoughtfully down at his half-consumed drink as he asked Doc Morrison whether his patient's cold clammy skin seemed dry and scaly.

The older man smiled thinly across the low table at Longarm and said, "I looked for that. His fingernails and gums look normal too. Where might a federal lawman such as yourself have studied arsenic poisoning, Deputy Long?"

Longarm replied without hesitation, "Riding for the law, Doc. You'd be surprised how often a mysterious sudden death turns out to be flypaper tea or rat-poison custard. You see, the stuff is sort of sweet, and so it's most often served with sugar and cream."

Doc Morrison snorted, "I know what arsenic trioxide tastes like. I know about the symptoms of such poisonings too, and what you seem to be suggesting calls for an immediate apology to your hosts!"

Longarm calmly replied, "I never implied anyone in this room might have been feeding Big Dick arsenic trioxide, Doc. There's a dozen ways a man working around barns, stables, and such could swallow something he shouldn't by pure chance. I just wanted to eliminate that notion, and since you say you don't suspect arsenic, I reckon I have."

Laguna Jacobs asked Nita in Spanish if she'd ever seen any arsenic flypaper or rat poison around the place. Longarm didn't let on he'd followed a ramrod's mighty fluent Spanish. Little Dick had, and asked Jacobs to find out whether there was anything like arsenic trioxide anywhere out back. But as the ramrod rose, Miss Aurora told them it could wait.

She explained, "We're about to sit down to supper, and nobody will be feeding my poor husband anything before I take some hot chocolate in to him later on."

So that seemed to be that, and nobody had ever sent Longarm down there to make sure nobody was poisoning a pesky unreconstructed Rebel in the first place.

Longarm waited until they'd gone to supper on the back veranda with the western sky blood-red and the too-sweet smell of some night-blooming jasmine on the evening breezes before he brought up the hired guns Big Dick had been recruiting before he took sick.

There was no getting around his having to ask, seeing the only woman present never left the table as the four men there lit up their smokes to enjoy with their after-supper brandies. So Miss Aurora was the one who told him, "I was against the idea from the beginning. As I told my poor hot-tempered dear, it sounded like a certain way to get poor Fiona killed."

Her stepson, Little Dick, agreed. "Made more sense to string El Pico along as you and the other lawmen, Anglo or Mex, try to get a line on the son of a bitch. Sorry, Miss Aurora."

The lady of the house just looked down at her brandy snifter.

Longarm asked, "How might you go about that, Little Dick? Might you have a mailing address the Rangers never mentioned to us?"

Palmer shook his head and said, "All the writing has been from him to us. We're still working on who he might have planted up this way as his spy. But he seems to know what's going on. When my daddy sent out the word about five-dollars-and-found for experienced gunfighters, El Pico mailed us from Ciudad Acuña that we'd be better off sending out of state for them *guns* he wants. Day before yesterday he sent us some *curado* powders and allowed he sure hoped Big Dick wasn't too sick to carry out his end of the bargain."

Doc Morrison asked how come nobody had mentioned Mexican folk medicine to him. The lady of the house sniffed and asked what sort of a fool he and that awful Mexican bandit took her for.

Laguna Jacobs volunteered, "I sniffed and tasted the stuff they sent folded in waxed paper, Doc. It seemed to be the usual *curado* medicine for bellyaches. Mishmash of dried cascara bark, chili peppers, and powdered pottery clay. It don't seem to hurt, and might do some good for simple bellyache. But I'd think twice before I chawed on *sugar cane* from any Mexican kidnapper!"

Little Dick snorted in disgust and said they'd already thrown the fool *curado* powders in the cesspit. Doc Morrison said he sure would have liked to have such a sample assayed in the hospital lab down in Del Rio, and added, "Might not be a bad idea to put Big Dick in the hospital till we figure out what's ailing him. I just can't say what he's come down with, and I'd feel better if we had some constant nursing and some other opinions on his condition."

Little Dick shrugged and said, "Don't look at us, Doc. We've asked my daddy if he'd like us to carry him into town. He says he has to run things out here whilst we're having this emergency about poor Fiona."

The big moose looked away, sort of pissed, as he added, "I'm going on thirty and my daddy don't trust me to brand a calf without him standing by to make sure I don't burn myself. But I reckon I know as much as anybody about dealing with Mex kidnappers."

Laguna Jacobs chimed in. "You start by shooting a mean Mex in the head to gain his undivided attention. The greasers who say they're on your side are trouble enough. What might this arsenic look like, Doc?"

The sawbones replied, "Pure arsenic is a metal, related to lead. It rusts in air to a white chalky powder that smells faintly of garlic and tastes slightly sweet. But I doubt you'll find any plain arsenic trioxide out here on the Lazy P, Mr. Jacobs. As this lawman says, it's more commonly sold as the active ingredient of flypaper, mixed with sugar and glycerin, or cooked into peanut butter and whole grain to kill rats."

Little Dick told Jacobs, "Never mind poking about for rat poison in the dark, Laguna. We'll ask the help and if they're on the level with us, they'll tell us true."

He grimaced and added, "If even one of 'em's a two-faced sneak, it's a waste of time looking for anything they might have cached on a spread half this size. I want you to go tell the wrangler I'll be riding down to Ciudad Acuña tonight. I reckon I'll ride that big buckskin Dandy."

He turned to Longarm to ask, "Could we interest you in a fresh pony, seeing you won't be taking that paint back to Del Rio just yet?"

Longarm thought before he decided, "That would be neighborly as well as confusing to anyone who watched me ride north on that livery nag. I reckon my own outfit can spare the deposit I left in Del Rio if nobody ever brings the paint back."

So Little Dick allowed that he'd go out to the remuda to help select the riding stock. As he and Laguna rose from the table, Longarm excused himself and said he'd catch up with them once he fetched his personal possibles from that guest room.

Nobody argued. But Longarm wondered why Miss Aurora followed him into the house as if he needed help in finding the place he'd spent his siesta in with another gal entirely.

Longarm had been raised to be polite. So he didn't walk ahead of the lady of the house as they headed down the dimly lit hall of her house. He figured she'd tell him what she had in mind, if she had anything in mind. He knew she did when she shut and barred the door after them in that same guest room. She was breathing huskily and her face was flushed as she said, "Custis, we have to talk!"

Longarm allowed he was listening as he stood a polite distance between the saddle over the foot of the bed and her heaving breasts. He was a man with natural feelings, and she was a full-figured woman smelling of rosewater and more musky body odors. But a man with a lick of sense knew better than to make a play for a married-up gal under her husband's own roof, even if she wanted him to. And many a total fool had made such a play when she hadn't really wanted him to.

He saw how smart he was when she said, "I want you to help me talk some sense into my stepson. I agree my husband should be in the hospital in Del Rio, if not the bigger one in San Antone. But Little Dick is so headstrong, and he was right about his father having to keep an eye on him around dangerous objects, like that brazen huzzy Fiona!"

Longarm cautiously replied, "I didn't think you cottoned to your kidnapped stepdaughter-in-law, Miss Aurora. But no offense, ain't this a poor time to be talking poorly about an abducted bride?"

The missing woman's stepmother-in-law said simply, "Somebody has to do it. I don't know what her game is and it's starting to frighten me. But hear me out before you and Little Dick ride south of the border in the dark under the delusion you're on some rescue mission!"

He said he was listening.

Aurora Palmer said, "Little Dick is a big kid who drove those cows up to Fort Stockton knowing as much about Fiona Maguire as that little fly knew about spiders in the song about the spider and the fly. I knew what she was the moment he brought her home to meet us, but everybody thought I was only a mean-spirited older woman. That shanty Irish army brat was older than my stepson in years and probably older than *me* in *experience!* Laguna Jacobs said he'd heard from some Mexicans that she'd been the play-pretty of a junior officer who'd been sent to another post lest her father learn of the affair and cause a nasty scandal."

Longarm cocked a brow and remarked, "If Mexican civilians had heard an enlisted man's daughter had taken up with an officer, you can bet your boots the post sergeant major would have heard about it, ma'am. So there couldn't have been much to such gossip in point of fact, and you surely know all you pretty ladies draw wicked fibs about you the way a pot of honey draws flies."

She smiled wearily and said, "Be that as it may, Fiona told me to my face she didn't want to go back East with her family when her dad retired. She said they'd be living over a saloon in a part of New York called Hell's Kitchen, if her father had anything to say about it. So it seemed obvious a discarded officer's mistress would have been willing to marry almost any white man out this way, and Little Dick is the heir of the biggest rancher for many a Texas mile!"

Longarm resisted the urge to dryly point out that Texas law gave at least a third of a dead husband's estate to his widow, no matter how his will read or what his other kin were expecting. But he figured she'd known that before a younger woman horned in on the Lazy P. So he just said, "Little Dick speaks somewhat higher of his Fiona, Miss Aurora."

She grimaced and replied, "Well, of course he does. She had him wrapped around her little finger *before* she got him to marry her, and you should have heard the moans and groans coming from his room the one night they spent here after the wedding!"

"Might you be in the habit of roaming the halls to investigate for such noises, ma'am?" asked Longarm, thinking back to that dirty chuckle on the far side of the very door she was now leaning against.

The lady of the house sniffed, "My husband and me could hear them without leaving our own room. My own Richard thought it was amusing. I found it disgusting. But that's neither here nor there. Let's consider why any newlywed with well-furnished quarters here on the Lazy P would want to drag her husband down to a stinky little border town such as Ciudad Acuña in the first place."

"Privacy?" suggested Longarm, as sober-faced as he could manage.

She demanded, "Then why not San Antone, or even El Paso, off to the west by rail, if one just has to poke about a border town for Mexican cactus candy or hot tamales? Why Ciudad Acuña in troubled times with Victorio playing tag with *los federales*?"

"Are you suggesting she was kidnapped by *Apaches*?" Longarm asked.

Aurora answered, "I don't think she was kidnapped at all. I think she had second thoughts as soon as she saw she and her sweet but not too bright new husband would be playing second fiddle to *my* husband and *me* for some time to come. I think she simply chose to disappear down Mexico way so she could run off with some other man. Maybe a Mexican. She's a Roman Catholic, you know."

Longarm started to ask about those ransom notes from a known bandit, and why a woman running off with a lover would be leaving messages for the law where the law might have never looked. But he never did. He was just as interested in why the missing gal's stepmother-in-law was so sure about a younger gal she'd just allowed she hadn't known all that well.

As if she'd read his mind, Aurora asked, "Which do you find the most logical—at least a dozen Mexicans, working rival market stalls but joined in some vast conspiracy, or a visiting tourist simply walking on in a crowded market whilst her husband's back was turned?"

Longarm sighed and said, "I reckon you know the old hymn offering the only sensible answer to that, seeing you're so proud of being a Protestant, Miss Aurora."

She favored him with a puzzled smile as she asked what he meant.

He said, "I ain't got the time or the nerve to sing it, ma'am. But the jist of the words to 'Farther Along,' sung in church or just riding alone, is that farther along we'll know more about it. So meanwhile, we just got to ride on till we arrive at some answers."

Chapter 5

Nita caught up with Longarm out back in the gathering dust to ask what he thought of the silk chemise she'd slipped in his near saddlebag. As he went on toting the heavily laden McClellan braced against his right hip, he said, "Ain't had a chance to sniff it. Are you sure it ain't been laundered since that missing redhead wore it last?"

Nita said, "*Sí,* she asked us not to. Is silk lace one must clean most carefully by hand with castile soap. She said she meant to do the silk stockings and underwear she'd worn at her wedding after she and Don Ricardo Poco came back from Ciudad Acuña."

You didn't tell one suspect that another suspect had told you that a gal who'd seemed so fussy about her underwear, and had set some aside, had been planning to run away from it. He just told Nita she'd been a real pal, and allowed he planned to come back her way before he lit out for Colorado, whether he caught up with the gal who owned the silk chemise or not.

So Nita told him to go with God, and skipped back to her chores in the house before anyone noticed she'd been fucking off.

He joined Little Dick and Laguna, jawing with an older Mexican by a corral gate. He saw they had a big buckskin saddled with a double-rigged roper and a Spencer .52 saddle gun, with a barebacked but rope-haltered chestnut barb of around fifteen hands awaiting Longarm's inspection. The gent who'd warned people not to look a gift horse in the mouth had likely dealt with proddy old Mexican wranglers in his time. So Longarm allowed the cow pony looked *muy caballo,* and draped his saddle blanket and McClellan over a corral pole while he replaced the rope halter with his own army bridle.

The Mexican wrangler and Laguna saddled and cinched for him while Little Dick bragged on how the chestnut barb had been swapped for two pretty fair scrub ponies. He said his own buckskin gelding had paid for himself tenfold, winning races with sporting men who hadn't heard about old Dandy.

But they never raced as they rode out by starlight with Miss Aurora yelling after them to be careful. They crossed the shallow braided Devil River and followed the east bank towards its junction with the Rio Grande or Rio Bravo, depending on which bank you were on at any given time.

That would have been about fifteen miles as a crow might fly. But they weren't riding crows. So it took them closer to five hours than the three and a half it might have taken a stagecoach. When you didn't get to change horses along the way, you rested the horses you were stuck with every three or four miles. Thanks to the cooler night air and the nearby water all the way, they could have pushed faster, and would have, had not Longarm pointed out they might want to lope those same ponies some down Mexico way before the night was done.

Riding easy, alone on the starlit trail, Longarm and Little Dick had time to talk more in private about his missing bride and the whole tense situation.

Longarm wasn't surprised to hear the vanished redhead described more fondly by her husband than her stepmother-in-law. It would have been disgusting to hear the lusty Fiona had been going sixty-nine with the gray-haired Miss

Aurora. Little Dick confided with a snigger how his blushing bride had produced a forbidden book about such lovemaking on their wedding night, shyly confessing she'd always wondered if some of those positions would be possible, but determined to save such experiments for her honeymoon.

Longarm never said he'd read the Kama Sutra with more than one other gal. He was certain Little Dick knew that no matter how many willing gals you read the Kama Sutra from India with, you just plain couldn't get two human beings in some of those positions, while some of the ones you *could* get into weren't as much fun as they looked in those sassy illustrations. There was no way on Earth to ask Little Dick if he'd heard his blushing bride had been used and abused by one or more officers Kama Sutra–style before they'd met up at that army post to the northwest.

When Longarm brought up the topic of his father heading for most any hospital, Little Dick explained he hadn't been the mule-headed one. He said, "My daddy's afraid that should El Pico suspect he might be dying, he might carry out his threats about poor Fiona. El Pico wrote us that unless he gets them six hundred Springfields and a hundred thousand rounds of .45-75, we'll just never *know* what ever happened to Fiona!"

He sort of moaned and cussed at the same time before he confided, "I swear, that notion scares me worse than the thought of Fiona being dead and done with! I mind hearing when I was little about this slave wench getting back at her master, or her master's wife, by vanishing with the white baby she'd been bought to care for. Nobody ever caught up with her. So nobody ever knew where she'd headed or what she might have done with the baby. She'd scribbled a note on the wall above the missing baby's crib. She'd wanted her white masters to know what her own black mammy had felt like when slavers carried her off from this African village when she was little. She'd wanted her white masters to wonder forever whether their pretty little daughter was dead or alive and how she might have died, or gone on living in the hands of *cimarrons*. That's what you call a runaway slave running free like a fucking Indian, a *cimarron*."

Longarm allowed he'd heard as much.

Little Dick repressed a shudder and insisted, "Study on it. Never knowing whether your baby gal had been murdered and mebbe *et* by pissed-off niggers, or whether right that moment she was chained to a bed in some *cimarron* hideout, forced to serve big black bucks like a whore, against her will or, even worse, *liking* it!"

Longarm agreed the slave gal's revenge had surely fit the crimes she'd seemed to be holding against white folks. He added, "That's one of the bad things about picking sides without thinking ahead. I read how this Dutch ship put into Old Virginia with no more than five or six slaves to commence the whole Peculiar Institution, and I doubt anybody there at the time figured on a whole great nation having to cope with what they started clean into these modern times."

He let that sink in before he casually asked, "I don't reckon you Palmers of the Lazy P might have any pissed-off former slaves for me to study on?"

Little Dick asked, "Why? Because my daddy rode for the South? Lord, we'd given up on the Peculiar Institution before we were raising beef this far west. My granddaddy wasn't no sissy Abolitionist. He just had common sense, and who with a lick of common sense would put a slave on horseback and arm him with at least a Colt dragoon?"

Longarm had to chuckle at the picture. He didn't have to ask why a working cowhand had to ride armed and dangerous on range so recently haunted by Comanche, Kiowa, and Kiowa-Apache. The Southern Planter had been forced to make some adjustments by the time he'd turned all the way into the West Texas Ranchero. Just as the Spanish Grandee to the south had been forced to treat his own riders more like men than dumb animals. There was something about putting any man aboard a bronc that inspired feelings of sometimes prickly pride. Or maybe it was simply true that no born lickspittle could learn to ride a horse worth shit.

As the two of them rode on, Little Dick asked why Longarm suspected some sullen servant could be up to no good back at the Lazy P.

Longarm didn't think he ought to mention dirty giggles outside his guest room door before he knew for certain who'd been out there. So he said, "I'm just trying to eliminate. El Pico could figure a heap of your dad's moves just from listening in as your hands, Anglo or Mexican, belly up to the bars in Stockton or Del Rio. But I'd feel better if I could be certain your dad's ague wasn't the result of something he ate prepared for him by a two-face."

Little Dick replied without hesitation, "The three of us, my daddy, me, and Miss Aurora, have already been over that ground, and it falls apart as soon as you study on it."

Longarm asked how come, and the sick man's son explained, "Them dry heaves and bellyaches first came over him on the way back from the wedding in Comstock. He thought right off he'd been poisoned. But like Miss Aurora said, none of Fiona's kin were at her wedding, and who else might want to poison any member of the groom's party? The church ladies who laid out the refreshments hardly knew any of us, and the old nigger who barbecued the ribs used to ride for my granddaddy and my daddy's always shook hands with him like he was a white man."

They were riding side by side at a walk, so Little Dick had time to mull over his words before he added, "Daddy's hardly et a bite from *our* kitchen since he got home from Comstock feeling poorly, and Miss Aurora makes the hot chocolate the three of us share in my daddy's room before we turn in for the night. Me and Miss Aurora usually wind up drinking most of it, and neither one of *us* feel poorly."

Longarm mentally counted on his fingers before he decided, "El Pico would have needed a crystal ball to see a rich rancher's son was out to marry up sudden over Comstock way. And even if he'd had more time to set up some wedding banquet treachery, we're left with one leg of the tripod. My boss, Marshal Vail, says to see who might have the motive, the means, and the opportunity. Or some reason, some way, and a chance to do the dirty deed whilst nobody was looking. There's no mystery when mortal enemies just shoot it out like men."

Little Dick pointed out that El Pico was a greaser, not a man as the term was understood where *he'd* grown up.

Longarm shrugged and said, "Leaving aside a known killer's manhood, El Pico's *motive* for doing your dad in eludes me. How could a dead man ransom a kidnapped gal with any-colored hair, and your dad hasn't been the one objecting to the same. It's the U.S. Government and El Presidente Porfirio Diaz trying to stop that arms shipment El Pico demands for your poor bride. It's been less than two weeks since she vanished on her honeymoon with you, and your dad has already advertised for a private invasion army and placed mail orders for Springfield carbines with more than one outlet."

Little Dick explained, "My daddy drew in his horns on the hired guns once El Pico wrote he'd turn Fiona loose for them old breechloaders. Miss Aurora said it would be dumb for El Pico to kill Fiona or any of the rest of us. She said we'd be prostrated and then nobody would ever see Fiona *or* them Springfields."

Longarm dryly remarked, "I suspect *probated* is the word she likely used, Little Dick. The younger wife of an ailing cattle baron would naturally study more on such matters. Should your dad die on both you and El Pico, the deal would perforce grind to a sudden stop and stay that way until such time as your dad's last will and testament, if any, could be approved by the state of Texas in what's called a probate court. Such approval takes time, and until such time as the judge says different, all the money and property left to anybody is frozen in place. It gets even worse when a rich man dies intestate, or with no last will and testament.

In that case the case goes to a *surrogate* judge who *figures out* what the deceased might have wanted, and whilst he takes his own sweet time and charges the estate a handsome fee for being so smart, all bets are off and nary a chip can be moved on the table. So why would any kidnapper want to harm one hair on the head of his victim's rich father-in-law?"

Little Dick said Miss Aurora had already pointed that out. Then he hesitated before he added, "Miss Aurora never really liked my Fiona. So I reckon I ought to tell you Miss Aurora suspects she was never really kidnapped at all."

Longarm was glad there was no moon up yet as he soberly replied, "No shit? Where does Miss Aurora think your missing bride might be?"

Little Dick's voice was hard to make out over the plodding hoofbeats on the dusty trail as he softly replied, "Run off. Miss Aurora says she could tell Fiona was having second thoughts over in Comstock before we were even hitched. Miss Aurora said Fiona was only out to snare a rich husband, and thought I was the owner of the Lazy P when I druv all that army beef up to Fort Stockton. Miss Aurora said Fiona's Irish eyes weren't smiling at all when she learned for the first time she'd be the *younger* Mrs. Palmer of the Lazy P. But why would Fiona go through with the wedding and damn near screw me to death if she was only marrying me for money I didn't have?"

Longarm didn't answer. It could hardly cheer a man in Little Dick's position to hear about other women he could mention who'd screwed *him* personally and passionately while trying to set him up for slaughter.

He changed the subject to learn the exact times he didn't have in his notebook, and so the conversation went on in to Del Rio. By the time they saw the lights of the county seat on the border up ahead, Longarm had determined Little Dick had started courting Fiona Maguire less than eight weeks back, proposed near the first of the month, and married her in Comstock a tad over two weeks back. Then they'd spent that one night at the Lazy P, screwing like minks according to Nita, and headed down this very trail to honeymoon in Ciudad Acuña, where the bride had vanished *less* than two weeks back, really getting her kith and kin, along with higher powers on both sides of the border, excited as all hell.

Little Dick suggested they spend the rest of the night north of the border, seeing few if any of the market folks they wanted to question would be up and about this late at night and seeing it had been Fiona, not himself, who'd been so curious about Old Mexico.

Little Dick said, "I visited Ciudad Acuña with my daddy and my real momma for the first time when I was too young to smoke them black Mex cigarets, and like I warned Fiona, there's way more action and things smell nicer here in Del Rio."

But Longarm pointed out that nobody had been kidnapped in Del Rio, and he wanted to start from that honeymoon suite near the hustle and bustle of the central market. So the two of them rode on to the south.

U.S. Customs wasn't interested in anyone or anything *leaving* the United States, and the more casual Mexican *federales* who usually kept an eye on the river crossing were busy west of El Paso, with Victorio on the the prowl that summer. So Longarm and Little Dick simply rode the ferry raft over to the smaller but more brightly lit Ciudad Acuña, and got rooms for the night at the Posada Madero, where Little Dick had stayed with his Fiona.

The Mexican word for "hotel" was *hotel.* Their word *posada* described what was more like a wayside inn, with a cantina instead of a lobby under the upstairs rooms for hire and a stable out back for the stock of the guests. So the street urchin being paid in centavos and smiles for such services explained that the two tall gringo riders he'd just seen getting rooms at the Posada Madero had ridden in aboard a *curtido* and a *castaña* barb.

The town tough he'd reported to, a notch or more up in the ranks of El Pico's men, went on fondling the *puta* he was seated with on a doorstep as he snorted, "Many gringo riders are tall. They get that way from sucking their mother's milk until they grow big enough for to fuck them. El Brazo Largo was riding neither a *curtido* nor a *castaña* when he was seen riding out of Del Rio on a *pinto*. So get back to the main *calle* and keep your eye peeled for a tall gringo on a *pinto*."

Chapter 6

Despite the hour and because of the way Mexicans coped with their climate, things were humming by torchlight in the center of Ciudad Acuña. So once Longarm and Little Dick had seen to their mounts and hired adjoining rooms upstairs, they headed over to the *mercado principal.* By another paradox of Mexican custom, the narrow aisles and small market stalls under acres of thatch roofing were as brightly lit at midnight as they would have been at noon, if not more so. So Little Dick had no trouble finding the leather-goods stand he'd been in front of when he'd first noticed his Fiona was missing.

But the young squirt with Aztec features selling riding crops and such said he didn't remember *el señor,* let alone some *señora* who might or might not have been there almost two weeks earlier. He explained he saw many pretty Anglo women every day, and hardly remembered the ones who *bought* something.

But they had better luck with that old crone selling cactus candy within earshot. Slightly better luck, leastways. The toothless old dear piped up to bear witness that Little Dick had been there, raising an awesome fuss, eight or ten days back as she recalled. But other than that, as she'd said on the day in question, she had no recollection of a *mujer* with red hair in a green dress. She said both the local police and later some *rurales* had been by to pester her about the same *gringa*.

The kid selling leather goods decided his uncle would have been the member of his family minding their stand that day.

Little Dick started to cloud up as if waxing to rain all over everybody. But Longarm murmured in English, "Don't get your bowels in an uproar, old son. If the kid wasn't there, he don't have to be lying. The old lady didn't have to say anything if she had anything to hide. She approached us. We never pestered her."

Little Dick insisted, "We would have. As soon as she spoke up I remembered her being there that day!"

Longarm shrugged and said, "Maybe you would have. Maybe she'd have just kept still, and we all look alike to them too. I want you to pay attention as I point out how tricky the light can be under all that primitive roofing day or night."

Little Dick glanced up, then insisted, "I don't care how bright or dim it might have been that day. In way dimmer light than this, Fiona was still a beauty with flaming red hair and a for Gawd's sake bright green dress with Rainy Susie skirts and yaller high-button shoes!"

"Let's ask further down," Longarm suggested.

So they did, with Longarm doing the talking, calmly and politely in serviceable Spanish, with things starting to make more sense as he was able to evoke vague memories of red hair here and yellow high-buttons there. A waiflike young *mestiza* wistfully recalled a *que linda* green dress she'd admired, but couldn't put it together with any other detail.

Longarm explained to the younger stockman, "You get used to this, canvassing out around the scene of a crime. Folks remember what's most important or interesting to them at the *time*. A newspaper boy selling newspapers outside a bank being robbed won't know said bank is being robbed until later, and meanwhile he's admiring a well turned ankle across the way, or hoping that dude with the three-piece suit headed his way wants to buy a newspaper."

"What has any of that to do with poor Fiona?" Little Dick demanded.

Longarm explained, "None of these needy Mexican market folks were here that day to bear witness to a kidnapping. They were anxious if not desperate to sell their wares. Likely just as worried about somebody stealing things off their open stands in a setup made for shoplift or grab-and-run. Anybody out in mid-aisle who didn't seem the least bit interested in their cactus candy or straw *vaqueros* wouldn't be of the least interest to them, no matter what she looked like. Don't forget, neither you nor Miss Fiona were *alone* in these crowded aisles that day. Other folks, Anglo, Mexican, well-dressed, shabby, were passing betwixt Miss Fiona and any merchants glancing out past those suspicious barefoot boys fingering the merchandise. Let's move over an aisle and I'll show you something."

They passed between two booths to the other aisle, which looked no different at first glance. Little Dick said so, and asked what Longarm was out to prove.

Longarm said, "Let me see who I ought to pick out. See that pretty *muchacha* selling perfumed candles two stalls down to your left? Keep your eyes fixed on her and smile as we drift in. But let me do the talking."

Little Dick stared hard at the candle-selling gal as he let Longarm lead the way. The girl was pretty in her own dusky way, but Little Dick saw nothing remarkable as Longarm stopped in front of her stand, ticked his hat brim to her, and said, "*Buenoches, señorita. Me llama Custis y estoy un diputado americano . . .*"

Which was as far as he got before the pretty Mexican looked up and snapped, "*Pendejo! No me vengas con tus penejadas.*"

So they did as she demanded and moved on.

Little Dick said, "I don't follow your drift. What was the point? I mean, I could see you tried to introduce yourself as an Anglo lawman, and I understood what she was saying when she told you to go away and not pester her with a silly line. But what was the *point*?"

Longarm said, "She'll remember us *now* should anyone ever ask her. But did you notice that before I spoke she never looked up from her lap? She's likely been reading a romantic novel, or else she's knitting out of sight behind her counter whilst she waits for somebody to ask the prices of her fancy wares. So tell me what she'd say she'd seen if your Fiona had been marched right past her in broad-ass daylight out in the middle of this aisle."

Little Dick sighed and said, "All right, now I see your drift, and I thought you'd been sent here to *look* for Fiona!"

Longarm shook his head and said, "They sent me to find out what happened to her and see if I can prevent your dad from ransoming her with all those rifles by any means that work."

Little Dick Palmer sighed and said, "My daddy's feeling too poorly to deal with anybody but Doc Morrison, and you don't think *I* would go along with El Pico's ransom demands, do you?"

Longarm pointed to a nearby exit from the market with his chin as he soberly said, "I'm hoping for his sake your dad will get better. As for you, she is your wife."

Little Dick protested, "I told you back at the Lazy P I followed your drift about dealing with El Pico. Might you be calling me a two-faced liar?"

As he led the way out up a darker *calle* Longarm replied, "Nobody tells the whole truth to everybody every time. It wouldn't be civilized. I'm sure there must have been times when Jesus of Nazareth told his momma she hadn't put too much salt in her stew. You seem to want your Fiona back as much or more as we don't want El Pico to have such a troublesome ransom. So we're on the same side but not playing exactly the same game. I got to assume you'd do most anything to get your pretty young wife back. In the meantime, I want you to assume I'll get her back to you alive if I can, but not at the cost of arming a regiment of Mexican bandits this close to the U.S. border!"

They found their way back to brighter lights, and made their way back to their *posada* for some sit-down thinking, seeing they'd drawn such poor cards at the market. They supped on tamales and *refritos,* washed down with *cerveza* at a testle table in an alcove off the main *sala* of the first floor run more like a tavern. Their barefoot pure Indian waitress in a ragged-ass Harvey Gal hand-me-down, was ugly as a mud fence and blushed like a dusky rose when Longarm referred to her as *señorita* instead of *chica* or worse. He sensed she likely felt like a Cinderella whose fairy godmother was long overdue and likely wasn't coming.

So when Little Dick left the table for a spell to take a leak out back, Longarm risked beckoning to the ugly little mutt. When she came over, looking worried, Longarm pointed to their half-empty beer pitcher and asked if she'd top it off the next time she had the time. She looked relieved, and allowed she'd been afraid he was going to complain about the tamales not being peppered hot enough for Texas riders.

Longarm laughed up at her, setting her aflutter, and confided, "I'm not a Texican, Señorita, so I ain't in that contest betwixt the *vaquero* and the buckaroo. I'd as soon taste what *else* might be rolled up in my hot tamales."

Then he added in a poker-faced tone, "That other gent I'm staying here with is from Texas, though. That's likely why you took me for a Texas rider. You recalled him and his young redheaded woman staying here not long ago, right?"

The homely Mex gal smiled, not a pretty sight, and replied, "*Sí, Señor. Con gratitud.* He was *bondadoso*, for a Tejano, and she gave me one of her perfume bottles that still had much perfume left in it when I did their room upstairs. I was wondering why she was not with her man this time."

Longarm said, "She seems to be tied up at the moment. The two of them were getting along all right when they stayed here, right?"

She said, "*Ay, sin falta.* They behaved as if they were on their *luna de miel,* and it was when she saw me trying to clean spots on the mattress she gave me the perfume."

Then, as if she realized she was talking to a strange man and not one of her pals after all, she blushed again and lit out, murmuring someing about fetching more *cerveza.*

Little Dick came back to resume his seat at the table, allowing he'd just had a look at their horses out back while he was at it. He said the Mexican hostlers had rubbed them down like they'd been told, and left plenty of fodder and water in their mangers. Somewhere in the night a clock was tolling midnight. So the trail-weary Texan allowed that he was stumped for anywhere else to look for his Fiona before he got some sleep.

Longarm told him to along upstairs, reaching for a cheroot as he leaned back in his seat and added, "I'll be along once I tell our *chica* we don't want more beer after all. It's been a long day, but what the hell, it aint *that* late and I may get lucky."

Little Dick laughed incredulously as he rose from the table to ask, "With who? Not that ugly little Chihuahua gal?"

Longarm shrugged and sheepishly confided, "She's at least as pretty as my fist and who says she's Chihuahua? The purebloods in these parts tend to be *Coahulla,* don't they?"

Little Dick shrugged and suggested, "Why don't you ask her? Fiona must have. It was Fiona who told me she was Chihuahua. Fiona was more interested in that sort of stuff than me. That's how come she asked me to bring her down here on her honeymoon, the poor little thing!"

Then he blurted out, like a kid who'd been trying not to sound like a sissy, "You don't think them greasers have been fucking her, do you? The Rangers told me El Pico would likely keep her safe and sound as long as there was any chance he'd get them guns for her!"

Longarm nodded as if he knew and said, "Makes sense to me, and you ain't helping Miss Fiona by picturing what I suspect I'd be picturing if I was in your boots. Why don't you get a good night's sleep, or at least a lie-down, and we'll talk about it some more in the cold gray light of rested-up reason."

Little Dick allowed that made sense, and headed for the stairs. So Longarm lit his smoke and waited until the homely little Mexican came out from the back with another quart of *cerveza.* Longarm knew she might catch hell if they suspected she'd misunderstood a gringo guest. So he placed a U.S. dime where she could see it on the table and asked if she could leave the refilled pitcher upstairs in his room for him. She allowed she surely could and scampered off, *cerveza,* dime, and all. Ten cents was considered a decent tip north of the border. Down Mexico way it risked looking generous to a fault. But he didn't care if they took him for a visiting cattle king. He wasn't ready to tell them he was a gringo lawman answering to the description of El Brazo Largo on those wanted posters put out by *los rurales.*

Knowing the *posada*'s tab for their midnight snack would be added to their bill for room and board before they left, Longarm left the main *sala* by way of the street entrance, having no call to tell anybody where he might be headed after midnight, with the well-lit *calles* still abustle but with the crowd commencing to thin out as it cooled off enough for serious fornication and sound sleep.

As he headed away from the brighter lights instead of toward them, he was being watched from a recessed doorway on the far side. The kid who'd first spotted him riding in with Palmer had been joined by that first tough he'd reported to, a higher-up who'd been told in turn, and a bitter-faced woman with a drinker's nose who claimed she'd once been spurned by El Brazo Largo and would never forgive or forget him.

So when Longarm passed on the other side of the *calle* she spat, *"Sí, ese cabrón es El Brazo Largo en verdad!"*

The urchin who'd first spotted Longarm riding in earlier with Palmer observed in the same language, "That's the one who rode the *castaña* with a *caballieria* saddle. I *said* he answered to that description of El Brazo Largo!"

The neighborhood tough who'd relayed this higher up in El Pico's organization chortled, "Is alone and headed away from street lamps or any friends to call his own. Why don't we take him right now?"

The older and more worldly *bravo* who'd brought the *puta* along for a more positive identification calmly replied, "There are many reasons. That is one most dangerous *hombre* for to take, and even if we managed to, he has many friends among those who follow La Causa Libre. So if *he* did not shoot us, who is to say *who* might shoot us?"

As the younger ones exchanged glances, he quickly added, "That is not to say the gringos can not be taken. The powers that be do not admire him nearly as much as the little people who would like to be rid of the powers that be. So why do we not tip *los rurales* off to where El Brazo Largo and and his so beautiful *castaña* pony can be found when he returns from wherever he thinks he is going tonight, eh?"

The kid started to ask a dumb question. Then he grinned like a shit-eating dog and declared, "That's right! He can't be leaving town on foot. So no matter *where* he is going, he is certain to be *back*!"

Chapter 7

La Blondita was either a whore or a heroine of La Revolucion por Libertad, depending on who you asked and what she might be up to at a given moment. The revolution against the Diaz dictatorship had been going on since shortly after General Porfirio Diaz, a hero of Mexico's revolution against the French-backed Austrian Emperor Maximilian, had stolen *that* revolution from the followers of the late Benito Juarez. In the meantime a lady had to eat. But very few Mexican husbands would support a woman prone to assassinate public officials, blow up bridges, or wreck trains. So La Blondita had supported herself as a member of the world's oldest profession until she'd made enough to open her own elegant *casa libertina* on a back street boasting neither lampposts nor a name. Folks with business in that part of town knew where they were going, and those who had no business there weren't welcome.

Longarm had business with the leader of a rebel cell, and he'd been there before. It was still a bitch for even a seasoned former army scout to find by the light of a late-rising moon. For most Mexicans, rich or poor, built their town houses inside out by Anglo standards, with the housing wrapped around a patio garden and mostly blank stuccoed walls facing the public rights of way. Rich folks up in the

States showed off their station in life with well-kept grounds, a fancy front entrance with lace curtains in lots of windows, and such. Spanish-speaking folks had learned before they ever got to Mexico that there was no need to advertise how rich you might be in a world inhabited by so many *ladrones desperados.*

Hence one narrow twisting back street looked much like any other, lined on both sides by moonlit blank walls topped with shards of broken glass set in cement. Longarm might have never found the place at all if he hadn't heard a familiar voice singing "La Paloma" somewhere in the night over soft guitar strumming.

That meant La Blondita was calling a secret meeting. You had to know more Mexican history than your average brutal *rurale* to follow the drift of that sentimental song.

The Emperor Maximilian, an unemployed younger brother of the Austro-Hungarian Emperor Franz Josef, had proclaimed how he just loved his new Mexican subjects, had managed to learn a few words of Spanish spoken with a High Dutch accent, and had had his court musicians play their sweet song about pigeons, "La Paloma," most every time he and his Empress, Crazy Carlota, had supped on the terrace of the palace he'd grabbed. So the Mexicans had known that "La Paloma" was his favorite Mexican song, and they'd played it under his window the last night before they took him out in the morning and shot him.

The song was about love on the wings of a dove, but the meaning it held for tyrants down Mexico way was clear to many an old rebel with bitter memories of how their revolution against a foreign tyrant had turned out. So Longarm drifted toward the soft strumming and defiant rendition of a song that was supposed to sound sweet. But he hadn't drifted far when something hard as nails and as cold as a banker's heart was caressing his spine while a thoughtful voice from behind him demanded, *"Que es la pasa de la palambra?"*

Longarm explained in the same lingo that he didn't even know the countersign, and added that he had other business with La Blondita.

The unseen gent who had the drop on him replied in English, "She and her girls are not open for that sort of business tonight, gringo. I am telling you as one who admires your pretty *culo* that you just may live if you would care to leave us your money and your pistol, eh?"

Knowing now that there were at least two of them, Longarm replied in a calm tone, "*No hagas fregas*. Gunfire this close to the *asamblea* is certain to draw attention La Blondita doesn't want, and once she finds out who you were shooting at you'll really *come mierda*! But mayhaps she'll sing 'La Paloma' to you before they shoot you. So what the fuck. I'm fixing to turn around now friendly as pie, unless you want to turn this conversation into *pura mierda*."

"No me jodas, gringo!" bluffed the one poking Longarm in the back as the tall deputy turned around with a thoughtful gun hand hovering left of his belt buckle. He saw there were three of them, all three in the charro outfits of top *vaqueros,* with cartridge belts crossing their hearts and *buscadero* gunbelts riding their hips. There wasn't enough moonlight to see their faces under the brims of their broad sombreros. He knew his own face was shaded by his less dramatic J.B. Stetson as he quietly continued. "That's better. I'd feel safer if I waited until you took me to La Blondita before we got into names. You don't *smell* like *rurales. Pero . . . quien sabe?*"

That worked. They decided no gringo had the *huevos* to evoke the name of La Blondita unless he really knew her, and his point about a summary execution was well taken. La Revolucion had no time to spare on protracted trials for anyone who fucked up.

They led him around through a maze of back alleyways and covered passages to a back gate, and from there to a spartan chamber furnished with a trestle table, opposing benches, a cross, and a tintype of the late Benito Juarez on one stucco wall. They knew better than to ask him for his gun again, but he heard the key turn in the lock when they left him alone there to wait.

Longarm fought the temptation to move over to the door and try the latch. Sometimes there were peepholes in a whorehouse ceiling, and he hadn't come there to amuse anybody. He fished out a cheroot and lit up. He smoked down five cents worth of three-for-a-nickel cheroots, and was fixing to give that fucking door a try when it popped open and La Blondita was standing there alone. "Well," she said, "are you going to just sit there like a bump on a log or would you like to come upstairs with me now?"

Longarm chose the latter with a gallant smile as he rose from the table. Most men would have at least considered it in spite of, or mayhaps because of, her official chosen profession. For she looked like a well-brought-up and mighty handsome virgin in her pleated low-cut cotton blouse and black lace shawl. Natural blondes weren't too common down Mexico way. More than one spiteful rival had intimated La Blondita's golden tresses sprang from a bottle. But her eyes were blue, and she claimed her momma had borne her to a Swedish prospector a spell back. How long back and how come were questions you didn't ask La Blondita if you knew what was good for you. So Longarm just tagged along as she led the way up a back staircase of the maze she did all sorts of business in.

The Mexican pal who'd introduced them the last time Longarm had been down in Ciudad Acuña on business of his own had said it was that impossibly innocent air about a lady of uncertain age and ancestry that had made her so rich so soon in a highly competitive business. La Blondita had confided to him herself that she was a restless soul who craved all sorts of excitement, but hadn't been screwing her customers since she'd set herself up as a *dueña de perdidas,* preferring the politer Mexican term for whores. It wouldn't have been fair to compete with her own girls, she'd said, even if so many Mexicans were anxious to fuck a blonde.

Once they were up in her room, dimly lit by perfumed candles, she bolted the door after them as she said, "I am most sorry I kept you waiting so long, Custis. But we live in interesting times. With most of the *rurales* scouting along the border for *los federales*, thanks to your Victorio and his Apache, and with the Yaqui boiling out of the Sierra Madre for to take advantage of the confusion, Mexico has suddenly beome the land of opportunity, and my friends and I were discussing the Banco Nacional."

Longarm got rid of his hat and took the seat she'd indicated, on her black brocaded bedcovers, as he soberly observed, "I met up with a Chinese lady one time who told me a Chinese curse went something like 'May you always live in interesting times.' No offense, but you Mexican folks might have been better off by now if you hadn't gone in for such interesting history. Like I tell my Indian pals, neither Victorio nor any other war chief is ever going to turn back the clock or even *hold* it long enough to matter. So what are you and your rebel pals going to do once they round Victorio up again?"

She turned her back to him to mix drinks at a liquor cabinet against the nearby wall as she sighed and said, "Go back to being whores and gamblers, or pretending to. If we can only manage to take three steps forward and two steps backwards long enough, one day El Presidente will wake up to find us standing at the foot of his bed."

As she turned to hand him his drink, Longarm said, "One day the old tyrant won't wake up at all. He ain't getting any younger and time and tide await no man. But I reckon I'd be impatient too if I was a Mexican. What in thunder's in this glass, Miss Blondita? It tastes like tequila mixed with white rum and . . . perfume?"

She said, "*Granadilla*, the fruit of what is called the passion flower in English. Is supposed to make one feel *romantico*. Perhaps it does. I have been drinking this *mierda* and having no romance for months, and in God's truth I need no love potions for to inspire *me*."

She sighed and added, "Was a *caballero italiano* I never met who told me is bad for discipline for to *chingar* with the troops. Tell me more about this *mujer china*. Is true what they say about the way such women are built below the waist?"

Longarm took another sip of the powerful drink and told her, "These other Mex citizens I was talking to asked me if it was true La Blondita liked it El Greco style. Seeing they were on the other side, I said I didn't know who they were talking about, but had it been that mutual pal who introduced us a spell back, I'd have still said the way a lady might or might not want to take it is not a suitable topic of conversation betwixt grown men."

He took another sip and added, "Where *is* El Gato these days, by the way? I was hoping this trouble out to the west might have drove him and his band back this way."

La Blondita shook her blond head and said, "You're no fun. Don't you know how easy it is for to raid army mule trains in the field for guns and ammunition? La Causa has all the volunteers it can ever use. *Pero* not nearly enough *guns* for to *arm* them!"

He said dryly, "So I hear. My own boss sent me down this way because of six hundred Springfield carbines along with a hundred thousand rounds of .45-70 that can kill at over a mile."

La Blondita replied without hesitation, "We'll take them. Name your price!"

Longarm smiled thinly and said, "A redheaded woman with or without her green dress on would be nice. But Tio Sam don't want me to get her back that way."

She said, "Custis, you know I speak English good enough to run a whorehouse in a border town. I still have no idea what you just said."

He sipped some more of her concoction—it tasted better as you got used to the smell—and explained, "El Pico has kidnapped a redhead from Texas. He's holding her for a ransom of six hundred Springfields and all that ammo I just mentioned. Your turn."

La Blondita curled a not-bad lip and scornfully replied, "That tub of lard who aspires to be known as a rebel would not make a pimple on the *culo* of a serious pickpocket. Is what your own underworld knows as a *punk*. You know how El Pico recently took care of a rival *ladrone* who demanded protection money from the same fruit stands? El Pico, the most dangerous one along the border, turned the *pobrecito* in to *los rurales*! We sincere enemies of the govenment spit in his mother's milk. We would glady piss on his father's grave if anyone in the whole wide world could guess who such a bastard's father might have been!"

Longarm drained the glass and set it aside as he said, "Be that as it may, you just raised an interesting point, no offense. Is it safe to say any Mexican gang leader of any stripe could unload a regiment's worth of guns and ammunition for a pretty centavo?"

La Blondita rose to refill his glass as she calmly replied, "I would buy them from the sucker of *rurale* cocks if I could not come up with a way for to simply take them away from him. You know what they say about politics making strange bedfellows."

But as she returned with his refill and sat back down beside him, La Blondita grimaced and decided, "*Pero no!* I think I would rather fuck El Presidente Diaz before I would let El Pico get in bed with me. Tell me more about this *gringa* El Pico is holding, the poor thing."

Then she set her own drink on the lamp table near the head of her bed as she rose, adding, "*Pero* speaking of getting in bed, for why do we not get out of this ridiculous upright position and discuss such a matter in bed, where I may be able to make you feel more comfortable?"

She was already shucking her duds, with the smooth teasing movements of a gal who knew how to make money taking off her clothes. So Longarm shucked his boots, rose to hang his gunbelt on a bedpost, and got to work on his own buttons as he calmly went on. "Neither the rich family of the missing redhead nor the government I ride for are out to save money by stalling El Pico about his demands. So there might be a bit of funding for your own outfit if you and yours could help me get the gal back alive. Tio Sam won't mind her rich father-in-law sending *money* to most anybody south of the border. Wall Street bribes El Presidente all the time and nobody in Washington seems to care. They allow it's the cost of doing business with you folks, no offense. So who's to make a real stink if Big Dick Palmer wants to pay a sort of finder's fee for his daughter-in-law?"

La Blondita reached up to haul him down beside her by his old organ-grinder as she purred, "Who indeed? Tell me more about this redheaded *crica* after you take care of mine! I have not been getting any of late and as I told you the last time, I got into this business because it seemed more like fun than work to me! *Meter palo* and let us rage together as one great upheaval of total depravity!"

Longarm was game for anything that didn't hurt, and Billy Vail would expect him to question such informants in as much depth as required. So he mounted La Blanca's rosy wriggling form and drove what she'd inspired with it to as much depth as he could manage between her welcoming wide-spread rosy thighs. You had to admire a gal who could blush all over after screwing her way to business success.

But he figured her feelings were sincere in the here and now. He knew his were, and as Miss Calamity Jane Cannary had morosely observed when he'd turned her down, it wasn't as if he was pure as the driven snow, and it sure beat all how a man could lose track of the cunts he'd been in and still feel the one he was in at the moment was the sweetest little pussy in this whole wide world.

Such deliciously deceptive feelings doubtless accounted for the way most folks from all walks of life felt about fornication, no matter how hard fornicating reverends and Congressmen tried to get them to stop. He'd once read an amusing piece about this bible-thumping meeting where a bunch of ministers had gathered to discuss all the reasons why the young folks of their congregations tended to stray from the proper path of Christian morality. They'd talked about lax parents, fathers who drank, and wicked French novels for a spell. Then a newlywed young minister had risen to ask his elders whether they'd ever considered how *swell* it felt down yonder every time you could manage to come.

So Longarm came in La Blondita, and not wanting her to think he'd gotten religion since the last time, came in her again before he asked if they could talk about that missing redhead some more.

But La Blondita didn't answer just yet. She couldn't, with her mouth full. So Longarm lay back and stared up at the ceiling while she gave him what her own folks called a *chupa como el amor de Dios,* or a blow job for the love of God. But even as he found himself thrusting his naked hips in time with her swallows, he caught himself wondering if Fiona and Little Dick Palmer had been doing this when first Aurora at the Lazy P and then the maid at the Posada Moreno had said they'd made so much noise. He knew it was all he could do to keep from howling like a coyote while staring down at La Blondita's golden tresses, picturing them red for added inspiration.

Chapter 8

The old fuss who'd first said virtue was its own reward must not have ever spent half a night with an experienced harlot extending professional courtesies to a friend. When Longarm accused her of just showing off in that one silly position, La Blondita took mercy on him long enough to share a smoke. But even as they took turns with his cheroot, she shyly confessed she'd kept herself going with many an ugly mutt in her earlier nights in the business by pretending he was handsome and that she really liked him.

He patted her bare shoulder and said, "El Gato told me how popular you'd been, working for other madams until you got so rich. The Good Lord knows I'm in no position to dispute his praise of you. For if you ain't the best lay in the state of Coahuila, you must be close to the top, and I'd fear for my spine with anybody better. But could we talk about El Pico now? How do you reckon I'd go about setting up a meeting with him, assuming you can't give me his exact address."

La Blondita took a mannish drag on the cheroot and handed it back to exhale and say she'd try. "If we who are sincere about La Causa knew where to find the big bucket of *mierda*, we would have fed him to the flies by this time. He hides among those *callejuelas* downwind from *la calle carnieria,* where few notice yet another stink. I can try to deliver a note to him, if you wish. I cannot promise he will get it, or know how to read it. Those forced to pay tribute to the *flojo absurdo* should be able for to pass messages on to him."

Longarm agreed that made sense. So La Blondita suggested that, seeing the matter was settled and he'd surely want to hang about until they got some answer, they might as well get some sleep before they got really down and dirty with their second winds.

Longarm started to object. Then he grinned like a mean little kid and declared, "Well, what Billy Vail don't know won't hurt him, and I still say this is in the line of duty once you study on it some, but I'd best get word to Little Dick Palmer, over to my *posada,* lest he wander alone looking for me and we wind up with *two* American citizens to ransom."

She told him he could send his fool message in the morning. But he handed her the lit cheroot and rose to gather up his duds and break out his notebook and a pencil stub, saying, "I want him to get this when he comes down for breakfast wondering where I am. I'm warning him not to set a foot outside the front door before I get back. I reckon it won't hurt for him to step out to the stable or outhouse, should he feel any need to do either."

As he scribbled his note, perched on a fancy stool while he used her dressing table as a writing desk, La Blondita regarded him languorously from the bed and sighed, "*Ay, que hermoso* a body you have. Do you train with heavy *posos* in a *gimnasio* for to keep yourself so hard and lean, *sonrisa de mi corazón*?"

Longarm laughed lightly and replied, "This sawbones wrote in this magazine I read that the only gents over twenty-five with halfway decent builds are either poor enough to work hard for their daily bread or rich enough to work out in gyms a lot. I ain't rich, and if I was, old Billy Vail keeps me too busy to spend much time at any gym. But I thank you for the kind words, and please don't tell me how *you* stay in such grand shape, Miss Blondita. Like I keep trying to tell you ladies, it can seem more romantic when you just take things as they come. Pun intended."

She didn't savvy enough English to grasp the sarcasm, but she left off asking personal questions, and rang for her hired help with a pull-cord next to the head of the bed. So a young *mestiza* gal trying to look like a French maid popped in while Longarm's bare ass was still hanging out, but just looked at her boss lady as if he wasn't there as he got all the way under the covers.

La Blondita ordered Longarm's note delivered, speaking rapid-fire Border Mexican that outsiders weren't supposed to follow easily. Once the maid left, they cuddled some and tried for some sleep, with her resting spooned against him as they both lay on their sides with his sated shaft snoozing in the crack of her soft but well-proportioned ass.

So when Little Dick Palmer came downstairs the next morning, he was handed Longarm's note. The big Texican allowed that in that case he'd have his *huevos rancheros* with a side order of beef tamales alone.

He'd just finished breakfast and bought a morning paper out front when he heard himself hailed by a familiar voice. He turned to see Laguna Jacobs from the Lazy P reining in a black and white paint.

As the big ramrod dismounted near the doorway of the *posada,* he told his junior boss that they'd gotten the wires sent from Del Rio, but hadn't wanted to risk wiring anything to a Mexican telegraph office. Western Union messages were relayed at the border to the nationalized Mexican wires. So Miss Aurora, back at the ranch, had sent Laguna in person with the latest news on Big Dick Palmer's condition.

Little Dick said, "I knew we could count on Miss Aurora staying a jump ahead of the greasers. Let's get your jaded pony around to the back and out of this sun. You both look like you've been moving hard and sweaty, old son!"

As Laguna led his lathered pony around to the rear of the *posada* on foot, he said Miss Aurora had told him to ride hard as he could.

When her stepson soberly asked how bad things had gotten at home, the older ramrod said, "Oh, your dad's feeling much better. So now Miss Aurora needs help in holding him down. He wants to start another war with Mexico. But Miss Aurora says you and that Longarm wanted him to sit tight and not do nothing until they heard from you."

As they approached the stable, Little Dick sighed and said, "I get the picture. My daddy has always acted as if I was too stupid to take a piss without hitting my boots unless he was there to aim my cock for me! Did Miss Aurora or that doc say what had been ailing him to begin with, *segundo mio*?"

The rider from home said, "The doc thinks it was something awful he et over in Comstock at your wedding, Little Dick. Doc says someone could have been out to pizen him and came mighty close. Doc tested a puke rag with some salts of his own he mixed up, and said Longarm had been right about some shit that smells like garlic."

Little Dick whistled softly and said, "He called it triple arsenic something. It's a good thing nobody but our own help and Miss Aurora have been feeding him since we got back from Comstock. I can see how she'd feel worried, coping with my muley old daddy and some sneaky sons of bitches out to kill him!"

By this time they'd made it to the open stable door. Laguna Jacobs asked how soon the two of them would be riding back, adding, "The lady of the house seemed mighty anxious, Boss."

Little Dick glanced up at the early morning sky and swore. Then he said, "I don't know how soon I'll be free to ride. Longarm never said when he'd be back. But he did warn me not to stir from here if I ever wanted to see my Fiona again."

Their foreman allowed he had no further suggestions, in that case.

Little Dick said, "I know what let's do. Miss Aurora sent word the hard way because she was worried about them sneaky Mexicans reading any wires before they were delivered. But what if you carried word from me across the border, even north of Del Rio, and wired home at the next trail town north? I don't see how El Pico could have anybody watching every Western Union office betwixt here and home, and that way you can rejoin us here by siesta time and mayhaps we can all ride back together, once Longarm tells us what he's been up to down here."

Laguna took a deep breath and allowed he'd best get started before it got any hotter.

Little Dick said, "Hold on. Seeing that paint's been rid some, and seeing you'll be coming right back, why don't you change your saddle to one of the ponies Longarm and me rid down this way. Both are fresh after a long cool night in their stalls. Would you rather ride my Dandy or that chestnut Longarm rode down on?"

The foreman was no fool. While he didn't share the good-natured contempt of Big Dick Palmer for his only son's maturity, he still had a sneaking suspicion he'd be better off lathering that chestnut instead of Little Dick's favorite mount.

So a few minutes later Laguna Jacobs was headed for the Rio Bravo aboard that chestnut Longarm had ridden in to Ciudad Acuña the day before.

Meanwhile, back at the whorehouse, Longarm was having his own warm breakfast in bed with La Blondita, the two of them being served by that same demure maid who kept pretending he wasn't there, even if she did bring two trays, pour two cups, and so forth. Longarm had read how back in the days of Casanova when French folks wore white wigs and fake moles, high-toned aristocrats had gone on crapping or screwing dog-style in front of their servants, as if they hadn't been there. He'd suspected, reading this, that that might have had something to do with the little people of France overthrowing King Louis so the first Napoleon and then Louis Napoleon could lead them off a cliff. But that was the way things worked, and he knew the oppressed population of Mexico was counting on La Blondita and her pals to make sure nobody ever did *them* wrong again. So while the maid was still in the room he asked his bare-titted hostess whether she could fix him up with some bloodhounds, or what she might call *sabuesos*.

La Blondita reached under the covers between them to feel him up as she replied, with the maid refilling his cup from the other side, "Give me the time and I can get you anything, *querido mio. Pero* for why do you desire *sabuesos*? They cannot lead you to El Pico unless you give them something smelling of El Pico for to follow, and if you knew for where you could steal something like a dirty *zueco* worn by the one you seek, you would know where to *seek* him, no?"

Longarm got his own hand under the covers lest she commence to jerk him off in front of the maid as he explained, "It would be way tougher to track a man I don't know through the slums in the lee of your slaughterhouse district than it might to cut the trail of the honeymooning gal he had kidnapped. I doubt he did it himself. A man who looks like a moving mountain should have attracted more attention in the main market that day she disappeared. But I got some underwear Miss Fiona wore up to the Lazy P before she came down this way. If I take me some bloodhounds over yonder and let them start sniffing near the leather-goods stand her husband recalls . . ."

The gal, who spent more time in Ciudad Acuña pointed out, "Custis, was days ago that woman spent a few short minutes in a most crowded market. Since then many others will have walked across her dainty footsteps, along with sides of beef, strings of chili peppers, and baskets of onions, just for to start!"

Longarm said, "Fiona Palmer wasn't wearing pungent farm produce when they grabbed her. She was wearing her own brand of perfume and sweating her own sweat through the same sort of underwear. I know a heap of Mexican folks from all walks of life have been over the same ground since she vanished. But how often might they scrub that brick paving betwixt the market stalls, and how many Mexicans smell exactly like an Irish-American newlywed who's been bathing with her own fancy brand of soap, soaking in her own brand of toilet water, lathering on her own brand of perfume, and doubtless having her own brand of body odors!"

La Blondita tweaked his pubic hairs and volunteered, "Not to mention other body odors a girl picks up on her honeymoon, eh? Is possible you have something, *mi amor*. It may surprise you to know we keep no hounds at all on the premises. But we shall see what we can do as long as we are waiting for an answer to your message to El Pico, eh?"

She gave the maid more orders in her rapid-fire underworld jargon, and added to Longarm as the *mestiza* left, "Now finish your food like a good little boy and give your *mamacita* a great big hug, eh?"

He told her to hold the thought as he washed down some breakfast with black coffee. Then he told her, "We got plenty of time. No matter how soon you can get me those bloodhounds or an answer from El Pico, I'm here until the noonday chimes announce La Siesta. You see, I've learned from past experience down this way that no matter how bad it feels, those dead-calm siesta hours are the best time for a stranger in town to sneak across the town for any distance."

The rebel leader sniffed and said, "Why don't you tell a potter how you make pots? Did you think *we* did not know *los rurales* pull in their horns at noon and seldom come forth again before three P.M.?"

Then she rose from the bed, naked as a jay but a lot more interesting to look at, as she set her own tray aside and proceeded to snuff out the scented candles, saying, "Is enough light through the window slats now, and will soon be too hot for serious *locura de amor*. Finish your *chingada* food and *chinge me mucho*, you cold-hearted gringo!"

So that was what they were doing, dog-style, when that samc maid camc in, without knocking, to sob, "*Ay, Dios mío—qué pendejado!* I had no time for to knock, *mi patrona*. I knew you would wish for to know *poco tiempo*!"

The buxom blonde blushed all over, but bit down with her innards and commanded, "Don't pull it out! She'll see your naked *piton*!"

So Longarm just stood there grinning like a shit-eating dog with his dong in her all the way, holding his fire, despite an urgent desire to come in the both of them.

As the maid busted a gut pretending not to notice a big naked man, her blond boss asked, on bended knee and with upthrust rump, what the hell the nearly hysterical younger gal was fussing about.

The maid sobbed, "You have heard, of course, of the *muy simpatico yanqui* who has fought for us, the one they call El Brazo Largo?"

La Blondita bit down teasingly on Longarm's throbbing erection as she demurely replied, "Every one has heard of El Brazo Largo. I have often wondered if he already has a *querida constancia*. What about him?"

"He is dead!" the pretty *mestiza* wailed, adding, "That *muchacho* you sent with a sealed message for El Pico just got back. He says they are talking of nothing else on the streets now. Some *vero cochino* betrayed him to *los rurales* and they set up an *emboscada* for to kill El Brazo Largo, and when he rode into it, they killed him!"

Chapter 9

That Scotch poet had been right about the best-laid plans of mice and men. Longarm had to make new plans, once he'd found out all he could from La Blondita's point of view.

Seeing it was generally agreed around Ciudad Acuña that El Brazo Largo was dead, Longarm kissed La Blondita adios after agreeing on a few other things, and headed back to the Posada Moreno on foot through the crowded streets of mid-morning.

At the *posada* he found Little Dick Palmer pacing his room upstairs, but when Longarm cheerfully proclaimed, "I know they told you I was dead, but I ain't," the Texan snapped, "I knew that. You just cost me a fine ramrod and a good pony. Laguna Jacobs came by earlier. I sent him off on that chestnut you rode down from the Lazy P. He was around your size and had dark hair and a mustache. So the rest is history."

Longarm shut the door and moved over to the shuttered window as he replied, "No, it ain't. I still ain't clear on just what happened. The way my Mexican pals tell it, a tall gringo led a chestnut pony aboard the ferry raft at the border this morning. Some *rurales* posted there must have noticed El Brazo Largo was even bigger than they'd been told, or mayhaps they just had buck fever. At any rate, they held their fire until the ferry was shoving off for the U.S. of A. Then the four of them opened up all at once to blow your ramrod, your chestnut, and a couple of innocent bystanders off the raft and into the muddy river! They figure the bodies ought to surface somewhere this side of the Gulf of Mexico in this weather. You say you sent the poor cuss off on that fatal ferry ride?"

Little Dick protested, "How was I to know them dumb greasers would take him for you? He rode in this morning with a message from home. I sent him back across the border to answer by wire. They must have been watching this place and confused Laguna and his fresh mount with yourself! See anything out yonder?"

Longarm turned from the chalky blue slats he'd been peeking through to say, "Not now. I naturally had some Mexican kids scout ahead before I moved in downstairs. If somebody spotted me crossing the border with that chestnut you loaned me, they reported it to *los rurales* and that was that, as far as they cared. Is it safe to hope the mistake they made left me a mount of Laguna's?"

The owner of all the stock they were talking about nodded. "His jaded paint is resting up out back with old Dandy. But dast we ride either through them *rurales* along the river now that somebody told them where we are and what we've been riding?"

Longarm got out two smokes and handed one to Little Dick, shaking his head and saying soothingly, "*Los rurales* ain't noted for complicated chess moves. If they thought there was anything about this *posada* they'd be interested in, they'd have arrived in force by this time. So I doubt anybody said anything to them about you or poor Laguna as he rode in aboard another mount. My Mexican pals suspect, and I tend to agree with 'em, that some ass-licking *lambioso* who knew me on sight must have spotted me riding that chestnut into town, reported that to *los rurales* for the bounty on my ass, and *now* the rest is history. I'm sure sorry about Laguna Jacobs getting killed in my place. But seeing he has, every cloud has a silver lining. Being dead gives a man with a price on his ass a certain freedom of movement down this way. You say poor Laguna brought a message from the Lazy P?"

Little Dick repeated what Miss Aurora and Doc Morrison had said about Big Dick commencing to recover from what seemed to have been attempted murder with rat poison or worse.

He added, "I have to get on home and sit on my daddy before he leads another charge like the one he led at Chickamauga. My daddy still brags about how many riders he lost under Hood at Chickamauga. I've also yet to figure out how we *won* at the *Alamo*."

Longarm didn't want to seem too eager. He knew the man was still missing a wife down Mexico way. But knowing how much freedom indeed he'd wind up with, riding alone as an official dead man, it was all he could do to keep from grinning as he soberly said, "If you leave just before La Siesta sets in, no Mexican lawmen tying up loose strings will be as likely to question a strange Anglo. With your permission, I'll move my possibles and your paint pony to other parts during that same siesta. So why don't we just send down for some *cerveza* and lay low up here?"

But they'd no sooner ordered some beer with some nibbles, when the same Scotch poet turned out to be right again.

The same homely waitress who'd just carried their heavy tray up the stairs came back to sullenly report, "Is an *india* in the back with two most ugly *sabuesos*. She says you are expecting the three of them. I told her *mi patron* does not allow animals on the premises, and she said she would hit me if I did not let her see you."

As if to prove her point, the door behind her opened wider and two mighty ugly bloodhounds barged in, sniffing and scratching, followed by a mighty pretty young gal, holding their leashes and dressed more like a *muchacho* than a *muchacha* in the white cotton blouse and pants, straw sombero, and rope-soled *zapatos* of the rural Mex *peon.*

She said, "I am called Perrita. I prefer to leave my family out of this. But my grandfather raises these, how you say, hounds of blood? So we felt would be more better if I was the one they picked up in the company of El Brazo Largo. They might not shoot a *muchacha* and I have been raped by *rurales* before. It does not really hurt if one does not struggle. For why do you need our services and which one of you is El Brazo Largo?"

Longarm decided her family tree had a few pure Spanish branches, but her big sloe eyes were pure Quill Indian as he smiled down into them to say, "Some call me that, Miss Puppy. My true name would be Custis. What might yours be?"

She sullenly replied, "Perrita fits my station in life, and *this* situation, better than what they wrote down in any church records. I am waiting for you to tell me what this situation is."

Longarm slipped the outraged maid a whole peso and assured her they'd be leaving directly before he told Perrita, "We're searching for a missing woman. I have a never-laundered undergarment of hers in my possibles next door. Do you reckon your fine bloodhounds might be able to pick out her scent from others over at the crowded main market?"

Perrita sniffed and said, "If she was ever there, Bruja and Brujo will be able for to tell me. But what are we to tell all those people when they ask for why we have hounds of blood sniffing through their aisles, eh?"

Longarm turned to Little Dick and said, "You'd best stay here and light out for home closer to noon. This young lady's reservations about a hunting party following bloodhounds is well taken."

Little Dick protested it was dammit his Fiona they were hunting for. But Longarm insisted, "Miss Perrita and me don't need you over to the market, and I have other Mexican pals trying to get in touch with her kidnappers for us. You get on up to the Lazy P and see if you can keep a lid on things up yonder. I'll wire you the moment I know anything, good or bad."

Then he nodded to the dog handler and told her to follow him with her dogs. They went to his room and he handed her the chemise from his saddlebag. As he led the way downstairs, one of the hounds poked the seat of his jeans with its wet nose.

Longarm asked Perrita to get her dog's nose out of his ass, and added, "If we say we're looking for a lost child with these hounds, the market folks ought to be *simpatico* but not interested enough in us to report us to anybody."

She grudgingly allowed that might work. So it only took them a few minutes to get over to the roofed-over market on foot, with a whole lot of Mexican folks shooting odd looks at Bruja and Brujo, if not at all four of them.

Once there, the hounds were less noticeable at any distance, but were making folks leap away as they moved down the narrow aisles. It didn't take Longarm long to get the hounds and their petite handler near those stands Little Dick had led him to earlier.

As Longarm talked with that same old toothless lady, Perrita gave her hounds a fresh wet sniffle of Fiona Palmer's perfumed chemise, and they proceeded to prove they rated the names they'd been given. Bruja and Brujo translated roughly as Witch and Wizard.

"She stood here for a time," Perrita declared as her bloodhounds sniffled and snorted the dimensions of an invisible piss stain only they could make out. Perrita added with a frown, "I fear you were right about how many others have passed through here since the woman vanished behind her husband's back. Sometimes, when someone stays in one place for a time and suddenly leaves, the scent trail they leave is not so distinct."

"You mean they're stuck? That's it?" asked Longarm.

The gal shook her head and explained, "They are hounds of blood. They think with their noses and the strong smell here, where she might have pissed down a leg when somebody frightened her, has them, how you say, distracted. You say her husband was over there at that other stand, with his back turned this way? *Bueno,* we shall move this other way, along this aisle until it meets another, and let Bruja and Brujo tell us which of three possible directions they took her from there."

That seemed to work. While Mexican market-goers formed a curious circle around the intersection down between the stands, the sniffing and snorting bloodhounds circled some, the bitch whined as if for mercy, and then old Brujo started sniffing the brick paving along one edge as the rest of them followed at a slow walk. Perrita explained in English, "They do not follow the prints of feet. As any living being moves through the air, *microscopio* flakes of skin and sweaty lint from their clothing is shed along with the odors of perfume, soap, and personal body odors. All this slowly shed *evidencia* drifts like most thin smoke in the air until it settles, as very fine dust might settle, sometimes many, how you say, yards to one side of the path they really took."

As Brujo swung toward an exit leading out to a back street, the girl holding both leashes as Bruja hung back, dubious, declared, "We had nothing worn by her abductors for to let them smell. I think at least one of them smelled very bad, to Bruja. Sometimes, when a *ladrone* does not wish for to be tracked by *sabuesos,* he dips his boots in spicy *salsa* or scatters ground pepper behind himself as he makes the tracks. Everyone knows that the slower the quarry is moving, the stronger a trail is left."

They got out on the back street. As more curious Mexicans gathered round to watch, Brujo looked up at them imploringly, and Bruja just lay down on one side to start licking her own asshole. So Perrita decided, "From here they took her away in a coach. Is possible for to follow such a faint trail out in open country, where not too many coaches have passed and some smell may drift down into the ditches by the side of the road. But here in the city, with every passing wheel stirring things up and scattering any odors left . . ."

Longarm said, "I follow your drift. Why don't we get these hounds and our ownselves off the streets before some *pendejo* in a big gray sombrero comes along to ask what this is all about."

Perrita gave a whistle, and Longarm followed as they headed for an alley entrance. Perrita said, "I am sorry we could do no more for you. Bruja and Brujo can only do so much and those kidnappers had some knowlege of *sabuesos*. Is safe for to assume you no longer need us and I may get home tonight after all?"

To which Longarm was forced to reply not unkindly, "I ain't half done with you yet. No offense."

"For why?" she almost wailed, insisting, "Brujo led us to the end of the trail. You must have seen Bruja was not that certain of *any* trail! We were asked by people one does not say no to for to help you see if you could track that missing woman anywhere here in Ciudad Acuña. We have tried. We have failed. I mean no disrespect, but I wish for to go home now!"

As they entered the shady alley, Longarm repeated, "I ain't done with you yet, Miss Perrita. I aim to pay you for your services, in addition to what La Blondita said your time and trouble might be worth. But if I was you, I wouldn't plan on heading home just yet."

The dusky petite Perrita kept walking in her *peon* pants while she heaved a sigh and said, "*Ay coño*, I knew you were going to demand I serve you with *mi cosita* as well the moment I heard they would be sending me to serve El Brazo Largo. I have heard the things they say about you and *las mujeres*. One can only hope they are not all true. I was a good girl before I joined La Revolucion and learned a *muchacha* with the right attitude could fuck her way out of almost anything."

When Longarm didn't answer, Perrita continued "*Bueno,* where are we going for such *acostarnos,* your *posada*?"

He said, "Just long enough to saddle a paint pony and see if we can't rustle up some riding stock for you, Miss Perrita."

She glanced sideways at him and demanded, "You wish for me to ride out of town with you? For why and how far?"

Longarm told her, "Can't say. I ain't sure. At least an easy day's ride to the west. Tell me something, Miss Perrita. Would making any lady change from a summer frock to a riding habit change her smell enough to fool these hounds of yours?"

She said, "No. Might be some confusion at first. But the longer she wore a change of costume, the more it would take on her natural odors. For why do you ask?"

He said, "We ain't licked yet. Fiona Palmer was seen over in the foothills of the Sierra del Burro and left us a message there. So it don't matter how twisty and turny they acted here in Ciudad Acuña, as long as your bloodhounds can cut her trail some more out in open country away from this madding crowd, see?"

Perrita must have thought she did. She nodded soberly and declared, "In that case, *vamanos pa'l carajo*. For a moment I thought you only wished for to fuck me."

Longarm started to assure her he had no such aim in mind. But then he began to wonder why any man would want to say a stupid thing like that.

Chapter 10

Longarm didn't want Little Dick tagging along, and he knew the missing redhead's husband would insist if he figured they might be on to anything. So he took Perrita and her hounds to a sidewalk *cafetin* for some sit-down *pulque con tapas* for the four of them. The amused waitress set out bowls of the tepid mildly alcoholic *pulque* for Bruja amd Brujo, but insisted they could eat off the dirt like any other *perros chingado*. She turned out to be right as the hounds slurped up their tapas as fast as Perrita could toss some to them.

Tapas translated literally as lids or covers. The ones you ate were snacks of this-and-that in a sort of envelope of toasted tortilla corn flour. The them-and-those could turn out to be anything from a bit of cheese to a chunk of ham, but mostly the chicken or beef they had more of down Mexico way. A dirty little secret of the big western cattle industry started by the Mexicans was that Spanish-speaking folks who could afford it ate pork, then poultry, then mutton and beef when they were forced to scrimp. Back in Spain they'd raised sheep for their wool and cows for their hide and tallow. A poor Mexican could still get fresh beef free behind many a bull ring after the bugle notes had faded and the *toreros* had all gone home.

But the two bloodhounds admired meat of any sort, and Longarm was only killing time with them and their pretty handler until that same waitress came out to tell them they were fixing to shut down for La Siesta.

Longarm settled up and left some centavos on the table as he told Perrita, "My Tejano pal should have left for home by now, and with any luck he's left me a pony that ought to be rested some by now. So we have to fix you up with a mount, and La Siesta should be the best time to visit with pals *discreto* and ride out to the west without having to answer too many questions."

Perrita pointed out that there were good reasons for La Siesta, starting with it being too *chingado* hot for horseback riding.

As he helped her up from the table, Longarm pointed up at the overcast sky and said, "Aw, it ain't that hot today. With those clouds so thick they hide the sun entirely, it don't figure to get much hotter than it feels right now."

She glumly replied, "*A, que gringo!* Have you never heard of our famous summer *temporales*? When such clouds move in from the *oriente,* is not for to dry laundry on the, how you say, clothesline. Is for sure much rain coming by *puesta del sol*!"

As they walked away from the awning shade of the *caf-etin,* Longarm said, "By then we ought to be at that other *posada* where Fiona Palmer was seen with those mystery men. In the meantime, we'll have spent the afternoon riding cooler than usual for this time of the year. On the map I figure we have a little under twenty miles to make by sun-down. So we'd best get started."

They rode out of Ciudad Acuña a tad after noon, with all the shops shuttered and hardly a soul on the streets. It had been easy, for a gal who lived there, to borrow a big Cordovan saddle mule with a center-fire dally saddle of the Mexican persuasion, its exposed cottonwood frame var-nished and waxed to where it looked like leather.

Little Dick and his buckskin Dandy had just left when Longarm settled up with their *posadero* and saddled the black and white paint he didn't have a name for. Like most cow ponies, it was a gelding of around fourteen hands. Longarm knew it had been pushed hard down from the Lazy P, but horses didn't sleep more than a few winks at a time, and by now the paint had enjoyed nearly six hours of shady rest with plenty of fodder and water. So he figured a pony in the hand was worth two he'd have to dicker for, and riding out on the paint with Perrita, he was just as glad he hadn't shopped about in a strange town for a remount. The chunky cow pony had to be reined in once they hit the open road under a cooler-than-usual Mexican sky.

Bruja and Brujo were in Hound Heaven as they got to run free off their leashes, with no tracking chores ahead for nearly twenty miles. They ran back and forth across the coach road in front of or behind the mismatched mounts of two far-from-matched-up riders. Perrita looked more like a young boy than a petite grown woman in her mannish outfit. But she sat her saddle well, and seemed to be enjoying the ride in spite of her moody remarks about the weather.

Longarm had no complaints about that cool, overcast sky as long as things stayed that way. The distant Burro Mountains loomed over a pretty shade of hazy lavender on the western horizon. It was too late in the year for the riot of flowers that could surprise the hell out of visitors in the spring of North Mexico. But as if to make up for that, the prickle pear cactus all around had commenced to set fruit. The Mex folk called them *tunas* and they looked like fuzzy green figs lined up along the tops of cactus pads like roosting hens. By the time they were ripe enough to pick, the tunas would be about the size of pears. That was why the Anglos had named them prickle pears.

Where that dominant breed of cactus didn't hog big patches of flat soil, where it's wide-spreading roots did best, the chalky *caliche* crust of the marginal range was mottled with a low chaparral of blue-green greasewood, dusty-gray-green sagebrush and spinach-green bayonets of yucca or the frosty green daggers of agave. The two hounds were going loco tearing through the chaparral after lizards and those big gray grasshoppers with black and yellow butterfly wings that buzzed like sidewinders as they fluttered a teasing distance ahead, as if enjoying the game they played with dogs and little kids.

Longarm and Perrita walked their mounts some and trotted them some to average better than three miles an hour while moving, but had to rest the critters, good, at least once an hour, which cut their average to slower than most determined humans walked.

Horses could run much faster for short distances and carry a much heavier load than a man on foot. But as all West Point cadets were taught in their first year, legged-up infantry could and often did cover more ground in a day, day after day, than the gallant cavalry. It more than evened out because cavalry troopers, or mounted infantry dragoons, could often get there first, and more full of fight, after sitting down most of the way. But things got less one-sided once you started talking about tired riding stock. Longarm could only hope the cow pony he was riding had been inured to driving trail herds slow, steady, and for hours at a time. There was less need to worry about Perrita's saddle mule. Aside from her being less to carry, another secret many an Eastern dude didn't know was that a mule was generally stronger and tougher than a horse of its same age and weight. Nobody would have gone to the trouble of breeding mules from ponies and burros if the resulting ugly brute hadn't made a swell saddle or draft animal.

Longarm called a longer trail break around three P.M. to water their mounts and both hounds before he broke out the trail grub he usually packed in the bedroll of his McClellan. The wind was picking up and blowing dust across the range at stirrup height. So they circled round to the lee of a pear flat to grub out of the wind. Pear flats were so called because prickly pear tended to grow that way when humankind let it alone. You usually got no prickly pear at all, or at least five acres of the stuff, spread out across flat caliche with nothing else allowed to grow between the three-to-ten-foot chains of flat cactus pads.

Longarm cut and peeled some cactus pads for their mounts before he hunkered down beside Perrita to help her demolish his canned pork and beans, washed down with tomato preserves. She said she fed those hounds once a day, lest they get fat and lazy, but they were allowed to consume any skittering critters they caught in the chaparral. That kept them from growing fat and lazy too.

So they were hunkered there, south of the coach road and out of sight of it, when first the hounds and then the mule perked up to stare through the cactus at nothing much. Then Longarm heard the sound of pounding hoofbeats and murmured, "Somebody else on the road this afternoon. I reckon I wasn't the only one who noticed La Siesta was a handy time to saddle up and ride down this way."

Perrita hissed as Brujo started to run off to see who was passing by. Longarm nodded and murmured, "*Bueno*. Why tell them we're over this way eating beans? Let 'em get their own beans."

Perrita said, "I like these sweet *tomates gringo's* as well. Is sugar they are canned with, no?"

He nodded and said, "That's why the label read tomato preserves. The sugar helps preserve them, see? I read somewhere they buried old Alexander the Great, or mayhaps it was Attila the Hun, in a coffin filled with honey. Not a pretty picture, even if it worked."

Perrita glanced up at the threatening sky to remark, "I just felt something wet hit my wrist. Was not honey. I *told* you it was going to rain and now we are *en pura mierda*!"

Longarm rose, muttering, "*No tengo razón—lo sé,* but we might be able to make that *posada* before it rains real bad if we hurry."

So they got cracking as meanwhile, up ahead at the *posada* they were making for, one *brazo* in a *charro* outfit of concho-trimmed brown goatskin came in from his post on the flat roof, declaring, "Is going to rain and that *gringo chingado*, El Brazo Largo, is not coming, I tell you. He would have made it by now if he'd left this morning before La Siesta. Where would he have been able for to hire a *caballo* during La Siesta, eh?"

His leader, standing at the bar with two other gunslicks, turned to mildly ask, "Was it your father or your mother they kept in that big glass jar because he or she had been born with no brains? Were you not listening when they told us he'd ridden down from Texas on his own *castaña*? As an *hombre* wanted as badly as us by *los rurales,* he would of course wish for to move about near town during the sleepy hours during the heat of day. If he left early enough during La Siestas, he could be here any time now. So get back up on the *chingado* roof! I am too young and beautiful for to die, and nobody gets to make two mistakes with El Brazo Largo!"

"I am going, but is going to rain and we are all going to get wet as the crotch of a *puta* when the *muchachos* have just been paid a month's wages."

His leader insisted, "El Brazo Largo is not one to be stopped by a little rain. If anything, he might consider it an advantage for to ride in through a storm. *Vete, mi pendejo raro*. Get back up to your post and do not come down again unless you spot him riding in from the east. I do not wish for to say this again."

So the lookout went back out into the dusty wind, muttering things about mother's milk under his breath.

The leader of the assassination team turned back to ask the owl-eyed *posadero* behind the bar, "What are you looking at, *mi viejo*? Have you never heard what killed the curious cat?"

The older man stammered, "I do not look at anything. I do not wish to see or hear anything, Señores. We are simple people here, trying for to lead simple lives in complicated times. If you would care for another round of drinks now,

I am at your service, with no questions about anything else for to ask!"

The leader smiled thinly and said, "*Bueno.* Go back to your quarters and fuck your wife if your daughter has the rag on. We have had more than enough for to drink now. I shall call you if we need anything else. I do not think it would be wise for you to take any further part in a little surprise party we are planning, eh?"

The *posadero* left the taproom without uttering another word. But when he got back to his family, huddled in the kitchen away from any windows, he was sweating like a pig and his voice was trembling as he whispered to them, "*Dios mio,* we are all going to die no matter how this turns out! They are here for to kill El Brazo Largo, and you have all heard what a dangerous thought this can be to have in one's head. They say he is a one-man army who never misses with a *pistola* that never needs to be reloaded. He is surely going to blow all these walls down around us if they fire upon him, and even if they win, can your imagine what the riders for La Revolucion will do to us if they suspect we had anything to do with this *chingado* situation?"

His only son, a boy of nine, volunteered to ride out to interecept and warn such a friend of La Revolucion. But his mother cuffed him and sobbed, "*Pendejo mio!* If you wish for to die just kill yourself and do not take the rest of us with you!"

Meanwhile, out front, the men lying in wait for Longarm were having a tense discussion of their own as the wind outside picked up to rattle the window shutters and blow dust in under the door.

A second doubter, peering out through the shutters into the teeth of the gathering storm, said, "If he was coming, he would have been here by now, whether he wanted to come or not. Is blowing hard enough now for to *sail* this way from Ciudad Acuña, and what makes you so certain

El Brazo Largo even gives two *mierditas* about this place to begin with?"

Their leader made the sign of the cross and sighed, "For why must I ride alone in a world of *nenes estupidos*? Were not any of you in the room when the *patron* explained? Is known on both sides of the border that this is the *posada* where a redheaded *gringa* scratched a message pleading for help. Do you think a gringo lawman such as El Brazo Largo would not have been told this? Do you think he would have been seen riding south of the border if he did not mean to search for that same woman? Can you think of a better place for to start searching than this last place anyone recalls such a woman scratching pleas for help in English on that *chingado* wall right over there? If El Brazo Largo does not come here in search of her, he is not really sincere about wishing for to find her. And as soon as he comes here, by day or night, in sunshine or in wind and rain, he shall die, for I shall be waiting here for him. And if you *muchachos* know what is good for you, you will be here too for to back me and my own guns up with your own!"

Chapter 11

Longarm didn't have to be told to come in out of the rain once it got to really gullywashing with the wind blowing fit to bust and summer lightning crackling all around.

By the time things got that bad, they'd made it on to another pear flat. Being from those parts, Perrita never asked what Longarm was up to when he led them into the sprawl of six-to-nine-foot cactus. She and her bloodhounds simply followed him.

There was barely any wind to be felt once they were deep enough in the prickly pear. But the sky was still raining fire and salt on them as he dismounted, unsaddled the paint, and set the saddle aside before he unsaddled Perrita's mule as well. Once he had, he gathered up both saddle blankets, shook them out to a wider single thickness, and forked back aboard the paint to gather in cactus tips from either side and drape already-wet wool over what would have been the ridgepole if he'd had a ridgepole handy. He pressed the thick wet wool down hard on the cactus spines to keep the gusting winds above the cactus jungle from blowing the blankets away. He got soaked doing so. But when he finished and slid off the paint's wet hide, he'd created a sort of miniature gothic cathedral nave about eight feet high, a fathom across, and nearly nine feet in length, with a mighty damp sandy floor.

He tethered the riding stock deeper in the cactus where they'd be out of the chilling wind if not any rain coming straight down. He cut and peeled some more cactus pads for them. They didn't need any canteen water, thanks to the juicy fodder. Prickly pear fruit tasted like a cross between figs and watermelons with a soapy aftertaste and way too many seeds. The flat green pads were consumed by man and beast down Mexico way, with humans preferring them sliced to look something like stringbeans and eating them like other salad greens with oil and vinegar.

Returning to Perrita and where he'd grounded their saddles, he found her hunkered down with her two bloodhounds, shivering and complaining she was wet clean through and just knew she was going to die from *la neumonia*.

He said she was likely right as he hunkered down to unlash his bedroll some more from his wet McClellan. The outer canvas groundcloth was as wet, of course. But as he unrolled the bedding with the wet side down, everything else was dry and warmer to the touch. That was why you wrapped a bedroll in a waterproof groundcloth.

Longarm told the shivering dog handler, "I don't want those hounds in my bedding, lest it stink of wet dog for days. But I'll turn my back so you can shuck those wet duds and get in betwixt the dry blankets to warm up. I'll hang your wet cotton spread out on cactus spines, clear of any more rain, and by the time the rain lets up it ought to be somewhat drier. It surely can't get any wetter."

Perrita protested, "You ask me for to go to bed with you, just like so, without so much as a tender caress? What kind of a woman do you think I am?"

He said, "A wet one talking silly. I never said boo about going to bed with me. Do you see me under the covers, drooling with lust for anybody? I swear, I don't know what gives you ladies the right to assume every man on earth is after the same thing, and to tell the truth, sometimes I feel insulted. So are you aiming to get in that infernal bedroll, or would you rather just sit and shiver whilst *I* warm up?"

She laughed, sounding sort of dirty, and warned him not to peek as she got to work on her mannish blouse. So Longarm gathered up his Winchester to mosey along their backtrail and see how safe they might be from unpleasant surprises with Quill Indians out on both sides of the border.

He got rained on some more, of course. But looking on the bright side, once he got to where they'd turned into the pear flat, he saw the pounding rain had smoothed the *caliche* to where their hoofprints were barely visible wet dimples in the temporary softness of what some called "desert pavement."

The almost constant dry winds between rains in those parts blew any fine dirt to kingdom come, leaving a surface of gravel, coarse or fine, but usually about the caliber of birdcage gravel. The dry spells between rare but really wet rains drew soluble ground salts up to the surface to crystalize and cement the fine gravel, forming a brittle crust about as thick as pasteboard that made for mighty easy tracking in dry weather. But of course all bets were off when another storm dissolved the calcium and alkali to start anew with a fresh crust of *caliche* from horizon to horizon.

Knowing the rain would smooth things even more at the rate it was coming down, Longarm returned to his roofed-over den to find Perrita under the covers with her white cotton duds hung up to dry on cactus thorns. He tried not to picture her doing so in her wet little birthday suit as he said, "We ought to be safe from your wilder cousins cutting our trail and wondering what we're doing in here. The rains smoothed things out yonder considerably."

Perrita pouted, "My people are not related to Los Apaches. Comanches, maybe. Yaqui, for to brag. But Los Apaches eat dogs and speak a tongue only they and El Diablo understands!"

Longarm hung his hat on a cactus pad and peeled off his wet shirt. That helped some as he said, "I follow your drift about their lingo. It's tougher than any other Indian lingo to learn. Some professor says Na-déné, as they call it, is related to the lingo of faraway Tibet. I wouldn't know. But it sure beats all how different folks have different things they won't eat. Na-déné speakers are willing to eat most anything that runs on four legs. Yet they can't stand fish, and our Bureau of Indian Affairs once came close to causing another Indian uprising when they sent a shipment of salt cod out to the San Carlos Agency to feed such folks."

He hunkered down to light a cheroot. The wet crotch of his jeans felt warmer if he didn't move about. Perrita asked how long he aimed to squat there.

Longarm shrugged his bare shoulders and replied, "For as long as it takes this storm to blow over, I reckon. It ain't as late as you might think from staring up at that dark sky. These summer gullywashers can blow over in no time, and seldom last longer than a few hours. So with any luck we ought to make it to that *posada* warm and dry, if not too warm for comfort, if we catch more than, say, an hour of afternoon sun after this gullywasher blows over."

She said, "Is going to last until nightfall. Maybe longer. When the *chingado* wind is from the east, the *tempestad* will stay for a longer visit than usual. Are you not *frio* in those wet *pantalones*?"

He said, "Yep. Might you be inviting me to take 'em off?"

She told him not to be silly. He told her she was the one who was being silly, explaining, "It can be taken as a given truth that most any man on this earth would make love to most any woman he'll ever lay eyes on, all things being equal with no devil to pay. But there usually *is* some devil to pay, and that's why good manners were invented. Human beings couldn't live together as civilized as Digger Indians if they didn't have some common-sense rules about *el rapto supremo*. Thou shalt not mess with thy neighbor's wife or any other gal things might get sticky with."

She pouted, "You dare to imply I do not keep my *partes* clean? I will have you know I wash, all over, as often as any *gringa*! Would you care for to *meter mano* and see if I am so, how you say, stinky?"

Logarm blew smoke out both nostrils and snorted, "If I was out to stick anything in any gal, it wouldn't be my fool hand. I've outgrown such kid stuff, whether you have or not. I wasn't talking about you being stinky or sticky betwixt your legs, Miss Perrita. I mean, you and another lady I've been sort of friendly with are members of the same rebel band. The old-time prophets who made up all those shalts and shalt-nots were roaming sheepherders who had just this sort of a situation in mind. Small tight-knit bands, standing alone against most everybody, can't afford killings or even fights over one another's *calor de corazón,* see?"

She sighed and said, "No. Who are your talking about, La Blondita? Do you think for *uno momento* she would even think of being true to you or any other man? *Jesus, Maria y Jose,* La Blondita is a *puta*! A brave one and a true patriot, is true, but nevertheless a *puta*! I think you must have read Don Quixote without getting the joke. That old man in rusty armor was a *tonto* for showing love and respect to the woman of the streets, Dulcinea. She would not have cared if Don Quixote had gone to bed with someone else for to keep from freezing."

He hesitated. She insisted, "Who is going to tell her, you? Do I look like a *tonta* who wishes to risk her wrath?"

Longarm still might have held out if, just then, Perrita hadn't laughed like hell and pointed. He had to laugh too when he saw old Brujo had mounted Bruja to rut hot and heavy as both sad-faced mutts panted morosely with pleasure. When Perrita said she'd thought she was the only bitch in heat around there, he decided he was as likely damned if he didn't as if he did. So he snubbed out his smoke, got out of his boots and britches, and it sure beat all how swell it felt to flatten out under dry flannel blankets, with a slightly damp but mighty warm naked female belly-to-belly with his bare hide.

She silently volunteered to get on top by simply rolling into that position as they kissed. But when she reached down between them to guide it in, she stiffened and exclaimed, "*Ay, que monstruoso!* Is no wonder you are in love with a professional such as La Blondita! How many women of virtue could ever take such a think up their *cosita*?"

He said if she meant to back off, she'd best say so before it was too latc to stop.

She laughed dirty and asked what made him think she was a woman of virtue as she planted a bare heel to either side of his bare hips and settled slowly down onto his shaft, as if she was getting into a hot tub. It felt swell to Longarm, and she must have liked it too, judging by the way she closed her eyes, raised her dusky face to the sky, and sobbed, "Oh, thank God my prince has found me at last and I find him *un amante tremendo y que sabe chichar como loco*!"

So seeing she'd gotten too excited to think in English anymore, he threw off the covers to roll her on her back with an elbow hooked under either wide-spread thigh as he took her up on her brag that he was a great lover who knew how to fuck like mad. He didn't know if it was her notion or not, but when old Bruja joined them atop his bedding with Brujo still humping her whilst she sniffed at his ass and started to lick his balls, he told Perrita, not the dumb animals, to cut that out.

He didn't ask her where her hounds had picked up such sassy habits. He'd had small lapdogs who slept with their mistresses act the same way, and a hotel detective had once assured him it was a sure bet that any woman checking in with one or more Alsatian shepherds or Russian wolf-hounds was surely servicing them in private for the same reasons few farmboys could resist their natural curiosity about willing female critters. He hadn't asked that hotel detective what had made him so sure, and he'd often wished he had. There was this famous opera star who traipsed all over with these two Great Danes on leashes, and once someone put the question in your head, it was hard to say you didn't give a damn.

When Perrita moaned she was coming while Brujo whuffed in excitement, he decided he'd wait until they were fixing to part before he'd ask if she'd ever entertained such notions. He was hoping she'd say no, but he knew he'd never forgive himself if he was still wondering in years to come. Back in Denver, some said his curious nature would be the death of him. But old Billy Vail allowed it made him a natural lawman, so what the hell, and if he wanted to picture a tawny little Indian gal as a taller pale-skinned beauty with red hair all over, it wouldn't hurt poor Fiona Palmer, wherever the hell she was, or who else might be doing this to her that afternoon.

In the meantime, off to the west, that rider who'd passed them on the far side of an earlier patch of cactus had reined in at the *posada* they were headed for.

It was still raining, but not as heavily, as the leader lying in wait for El Brazo Largo ordered tequila all around and got their wet *compañero* in front of a roaring fire on a corner hearth. The leader observed, "You look like a drowned rat. What was so important it could not wait out this storm, eh?"

The new arrival removed his soggy sombrero and *charro* jacket as he replied, "Was not raining when I left Ciudad Acuña. Was more than halfway when it started, and I knew our *patron* would not wish for me to turn back in any case. He said his message about El Brazo Largo was of great importance."

The team leader swore and said, "*Bueno*. So what is this great message? Are we supposed to guess or would you care to tell us in your own good time? Spit it out, you *tonto loco*!"

So the dispatch rider answered simply, "El Brazo Largo is dead. *Los rurales* got him this morning at the river crossing, and you should hear them bragging. *Los rurales* think they are so smart. As if the robbing of a poor box or the rape of one's little sister was a big accomplishment."

Their leader snapped, "Never mind all that. Everyone knows what those fuckers of their mothers are like. Tell us how they got El Brazo Largo! How many *rurales* did he take with him?"

The rider from town shrugged and said, "None. Has ever been thus when the great fighters die. Great fighters do not die unless they never see it coming. They let that big Yanqui go aboard the ferry as if they suspected nothing. Then, as the ferry raft shoved off, they let him have it. They filled him so full of lead he may never come up from the river bottom now. *El patron* said you would wish for to know. I think he may have better things for you to do, now that he no longer has to worry about El Brazo Largo."

One of the others suggested, "Let us kill the *posadero* with his his family and ride, no?"

The team leader stepped over to the window to peer out as he said, "Let us all shut our mouths and give a man time for to think, eh? Is still raining hard outside. Many arroyos will be flood long after the rain lets up. Don't kill anybody until I decide whether we should stay the night or not. Dead men tell no tales, is true, but dead men serve no drinks, and dead women are not much fun for to fuck either."

Chapter 12

By five that afternoon the wind had shifted, becoming warmer and drier from the southwest and blowing the rain up Texas way. So that felt swell. Then the sun came back out to turn their cactus patch into a steam bath that felt awful. So they put on their still-damp duds, saddled up, and rode on, with two bloodhounds less interested in rutting or chasing lizards as the afternoon on the trail wore on.

They'd topped their canteens during the summer storm, and only had a few more miles to go. But Longarm advised, and Perrita agreed, that they ought to husband their water and give what they could spare to their mounts during trail breaks. A human sitting down could have made it all the way from Ciudad Acuña to the Burros without a single drink of water, although they'd have wound up willing to sell their souls for a cold beer before they reached that *posada*. But horses and even mules just dropped dead, all of a sudden, when they got too dry. Not being able to talk and not feeling up to bucking when they were really feeling bad, they had no way to tell you they were dying until they just upped and died.

This had only happened to Longarm a few times. Such unpleasant surprises had taught him to look out for literally dumb animals. The two bloodhounds could look after themselves almost as well as cats, a dog being much smarter than any horse outside a sentimental novel such as *Black Beauty*.

Longarm and Perrita were wishing that the overcast sky would come back, even if it meant more rain, by the time they'd left the last pear flats behind, with the range all around commencing to roll like the groundswells of a chaparral-covered sea. The chaparral was getting higher too, as greasewood and sage gave way to catclaw, paloverde, and such, with all of it wet and the late sun in a cloudless sky beaming down on the soggy bare soil between. So the humid air felt hotter than it was, and you couln't make out the mountains rising to the west, even though they had to be much nearer now.

It was in such misty light, with the rays slanting seriously from the the west, that the four *buscaderos* who'd given up on waiting at that *posada* topped a rise to find themselves staring at two other riders, a tall gringo and a petite *peon,* who'd reined in atop the next rise to the east.

From where Longarm and Perrita had been alerted by the bloodhounds that something awful lay out ahead, the four Mexicans were just black outlines wearing broad sombreros. But Longarm had thoughtfully drawn his Winchester from its saddle boot to rest across his thighs, with a round in the chamber.

The odds were still four to one, since Perrita wasn't armed with anything but her barlow knife, and so one of the Mexicans declared to the others. Then he added, "Nice pinto, and I claim his boots because I saw them first."

Their leader said, just loud enough for them to hear, "*No hagas fregas*. Let them come to us. I will fire when I think is the right time. Try not to kill the little one. I think that may be a *muchacha* and as I keep telling you, is no fun for to fuck a dead woman."

But Longarm had no mind to ride across that draw and upslope toward four unknown riders with the sun at their backs and full in his face. So he told Perrita to stay on the far side of him as he reined off the coach road through the high chaparral, winking in and out of sight from the riders along that rise, and vice versa.

"Ay maricón, a 'onde va?" yelled the leader as Longarm and Perrita just kept sidewinding without answering. For when a stranger called you a sissy and asked where you were headed, you didn't owe him any answer.

The riders on the ridge began to inch their own mounts to the north apace with Longarm and Perrita, calling out repeated rude invitations to stop and chat. The Mexicans were confident because they had no idea who Longarm was, seeing El Brazo Largo had been killed by *los rurales,* and they were sure they could outride any gringo on their own familiar range. They weren't too worried about the saddle gun their intended victim had drawn. Their own carbines were riding across their own knees and there were four of them. With any luck the gringo would see it was hopeless and give in without a fight, hoping to at least escape with his life.

He wasn't going to, of course. But why spoil a nice surprise by giving it away too soon? The leader called out in passable English. "Hey, gringo, I am talking to you! For why you so stuck up? You wish for to make us mad at you?"

Longarm reined in, telling Perrita, "They're getting set for a showdown, girl. Flatten across your saddlehorn and beeline for home at a dead run without looking back. What are you waiting for? *Vente, mi querida!*"

So Perrita lit out followed by her bloodhounds, as Longarm got set for what had to happen next.

What happened next wasn't what the overconfident riders off to his west had been expecting. The first thing tipping the odds a tad in the favor of an outnumbered rider was that they didn't know who he was. He didn't know who they were either, but had the added advantage of not feeling better than gents he didn't know. After that, their four-to-one advantage in saddle guns just wasn't there.

Like most Mexican outlaws, they'd armed themselves with weapons stolen from soldiers or lawmen armed by the Mexican Government, led by a lone autocrat who just admired the shit out of the U.S. Army.

That was the reason El Pico was holding out for that ransom of U.S. Army Springfield .45-70's and why the four riders were fixing to fight it out with four Springfields against a Winchester '73 throwing .44-40.

The U.S. Army-issue .45-70 round was a man-killing pisser at longer range than the .44-40's Longarm loaded in both his side arm and saddle gun. But they weren't confronting one another at such long range, and another good reason to settle on what seemed a mighty jolting pistol round and a lukewarm rifle round was that the same .44-40 cartridge fired from two very different guns gave very different results.

Forty grains of powder, trying to push a .44 slug, lost a good bit of pressure as visible side-flash and gunsmoke out the gap between the cylinder and the barrel. And the barrel of any six-gun was too short to hold most of the expanding gas before the bullet left the muzzle to be on its way. So the effective range of a .44-40 *six-gun* was fifty yards with accuracy, and a hundred yards with luck. While the same .44-40 round, fired from a carbine with no side-flash loss and almost two feet of barrel for the gas to expand in, pushed two hundred grains of lead two hundred yards flat out, with elevation offering a fair chance of hitting the target at four hundred.

The riders blocking his way west might or might not have known this. Their own Springfields threw bigger bullets over twice as far.

But they fired single-shot, and Longarm figured the range at less than two hundred yards as he responded to, "What's the matter, gringo, has the cat got your tongue?" by firing first, and then firing some more, as fast as he could lever the action of his repeating carbine while only one of the taunting Mexicans managed to fire into the cloud of gunsmoke where their intended victim had just seemed to cower silently in the saddle.

It was easier to aim through gunsmoke at black outlines against a sunset sky, so Longarm emptied four saddles at the rate he could have counted to that number out loud, before he swung easily to the *caliche* to tether his mount to some mesquite.

That was when he noticed the horse was bleeding. They called horses dumb brutes with good reason. The ancient Romans had been able to stop charging elephants just by standing their ground and banging their brass shields. But those fine cavalry mounts had carried the Light Brigade right into the jaws of Hell in that Crimean War. So even as he asked the poor paint how bad it was, the pony seemed to deflate like a punctured water bag and collapse in the chaparral.

He turned as Perrita called out to him. She'd turned her mule to ride back. A bloodhound preceded her through the chapparal to whuff and sniffle from one end of the dead horse to the other. Longarm said, "He took some .45-70 through the lung, and get your nose out of his ass, Bruja. That's disgusting."

He was reloading his Winchester as the gal joined him, asking what all that had been about. He replied, "Don't know. Stay here whilst I can see if I can find out. I'm scouting ahead on foot for any of the sons of bitches laying doggo in the sticker bush."

He moved across the shallow draw and up the next rise behind the sniffing muzzle of his Winchester. As he did so he saw two of their ponies were still standing, rein-trained, as many Mexican ponies were, to stand in place once their reins were dragging on the ground. Few *vaqueros* tied the ends of their reins together to keep from dropping one at an awkward moment. The mostly Indian Mexican *vaqueros* had been trained by Spanish riding masters, and Spain was still famous for its riding-school *dressage* classes, where neither the mount nor its rider was allowed to make the least mistake.

One of the still-standing ponies had taken one of Longarm's .44 slugs in the throat, to stand there gurgling while it waited for somebody to do something about that. Longarm called out that he'd be there directly. The four men he'd shot were of more concern to him than a shot-up pony.

He started finding them about where he'd seen them drop in the high chapparal along the rise. All of them were dressed like prosperous *vaqueros,* or show-off *banditos,* in leather *charro* outfits with brocaded sombreros and tooled, silver-mounted gunbelts, packing the Colt '73 Peacemakers so popular down Mexico way.

One was still alive. Sort of. As Longarm hunkered down to feel the side of his throat, the shot-up Mexican opened his eyes to gently smile and weakly mutter, "Hey, you are pretty good, gringo. How are you called?"

Longarm calmly replied, "They call me El Brazo Largo. Were you four riding for El Pico or did we just look tempting?"

The dying Mex asked innocently, "Who is this El Pico? I have never heard of him. And how could you be El Brazo Largo? El Brazo Largo is no more. He was killed this very morning. Had you not heard?"

Longarm dryly replied, "Seems I did hear words to that effect back in town, now that you mention it. What can you tell me about that redhead El Pico has been holding?"

The dying man didn't answer. He'd finished dying. Longarm stood up to wave Perrita in before he gingerly eased along the rise toward the standing pony that didn't seem hurt. It was a dark palomino mare, with an almost fawn hide contrasting with its flaxen mane and tail. She showed some white to her eye as Longarm made a last sudden lunge for her dangling reins, but didn't fight him as he tethered her more securely to some waist-high catclaw.

He was headed for the roan hit in the throat as Perrita reined in nearby to call out to him again.

He called back, "You'd best get set for some shying, or better yet, dismount whilst I take care of this hurt horse. I doubt a vet could save it if we were back in town. But it figures to drown slow on its own blood if I don't ease it on over the divide."

The Indian gal slid off her mule behind him as Longarm strode on to the pony he'd shot to shoot it some more with a merciful round in its brain.

The sun was fixing to set by the time they'd gone through pockets and saddlebags, fetched Longarm's saddle and saddlebags from the dead paint across the way, and rode on, with Perrita now sporting two saddlebags filled with silver conchos and loose change, armed to her pretty teeth with the prettiest brace of silver-mounted six-guns in a tooled and silver-mounted gunbelt, with the other guns and ammunition wrapped in the bedroll tarp of a dead man and buried where Perrita's pals, but not their own, would be able to salvage them later.

They spied the wayside *posada* up ahead by the last fading light of the gloaming. Perrita said, "I wonder for why is so dark? They should have lit at least some candles inside by this time, no?"

Longarm reined in as he replied, "I noticed. You're right. Stay here and hold these reins for me, *por favor, querida.* I'd best scout ahead some."

He tried to. But the two bloodhounds went sniffing well in front of him, until Bruja suddenly sat down to howl and Brujo turned back to stare up at Longarm with a mighty worried expression, even for a bloodhound.

Longarm called ahead. He got no answer. He moved in out of line with the front door, got a blind corner between himself and anyone inside, and chased the muzzle of his Winchester over to flatten out against a 'dobe wall and inch his way to an open window.

He risked a quick peek, swore, and took a longer look into what seemed a Mexican version of the last act of *Hamlet*.

As he counted the still forms sprawled across the tile floor inside, with the twilight from outside turning those pools of blood into puddles of jet-black ink, he made them to be four, a middle-aged man, a not-much-younger woman, an older woman, and a boy of about nine. He moved around to the rear door and worked his way forward through every room before calling Perrita in.

He found the dead girl of about fourteen face up and stark naked across a rumpled bed, with four bullet holes in her slim young body and the sheets soaked with her blood. Her blouse and dress lay near the foot of the bed on the floor. A man's bloody boot print stood out againt the white cotton of her blouse. There were no other dead folks on the premises. The dead dog that had upset the bloodhounds lay behind the bar out front. The trail of blood droplets could be read to tell a tale of a family pet doing its best and crawling for cover after it had been shot more than once.

Longarm opened the front door and stepped out to call Perrita in. As she and her mule led his fresh palomino up to the hitching rail in the dooryard, Perrita asked if he'd found out why it was so dark inside.

To which Longarm could only reply, "I have, and I sure wish those four sons of bitches could have taken longer to die. Let me help you with those reins. We'd best tether both brutes tight. Critters can be mighty unsettled by the smell of blood and we got more than enough of that to clean up inside."

Chapter 13

It was a tough, dirty job, but somebody had to do it in such hot and sticky weather. The Mexican summer sun was going to take a spell to repave the semi-desert with *caliche* and get the chaparral to smell like medicine for colds some more, and they didn't have a root cellar or a smokehouse.

The digging would have been easier outside after all that rain, for coyotes as well as a neighborly gent with a shovel. But Longarm was able to get going in a dirt-floored pantry off the kitchen, once he got down through earth packed hard by generations of bare feet.

The subsoil was mostly clay and he was glad. He explained why to Perrita as she helped him wrap the bodies in bedding once he'd rinsed them off with pump water. Bodies buried in damp clay kept surprisingly long because most decay bugs needed some air. He explained as they laid the family of five in their shallow bed of clay that he only wanted to bury them deep enough to keep until their kith and kin could be told and their church could rebury them more formally.

As he shoveled granular clay back into the shallow grave to hide the already oozing bundles of bedding, Perrita asked, "What about the poor horses and those wicked killers off to the east?"

Longarm said, "The buzzards circling in the morning ought to draw any *rurale* patrols in these parts. Once they find them shot-up sons of bitches, they ought to head on over here, and I mean to leave them a note explaining what we just done here and why we had to do it. I don't reckon I ought to sign my name, seeing they'd feel so hurt if they found out they hadn't killed me after all."

He set the shovel against a wall and added, "That's enough for now. We've other fish to fry, and I'll fetch some water in here as soon as my back feels up to it. Where have your bloodhounds gone now? I have a chore for 'em."

Perrita whistled and Bruja and Brujo came in, looking guilty about something. Longarm figured they'd likely been licking up blood. He'd tossed that dead dog in the hole first.

Once Longarm explained what he wanted, Perrita took out the underwear once worn by the missing Fiona Palmer and let both hounds slobber it before she hissed, "*Vamos a buscar. Por donde está la mujer?*"

So the bloodhounds commenced to sniff all over, stopping now and again to stare back reproachfully as if unsettled by all the wilder smells of blood and gunsmoke, until they finally worked their way to a corner table out front, where Brujo whimpered and Bruja bayed at the ceiling.

Longarm moved the small blue table aside, and hunkered down to run his fingertips over what felt like fresh plaster as he nodded and told the hound's handlers, "The police reports I read allowed it was in this corner that a redheaded Anglo woman scratched a plea for help and said they were taking her on to that Escondijo Yaqui. But how can we be sure your dogs are sure? They don't look too sure to me, no offense."

Perrita said, "They would not look at all sure if there was not some trace of her odor left in that corner. You forget this is a public wayside stop. Any number of other men and women will have spent as much or more time at that table, and that was before this whole place was made for to reek of blood, gunsmoke, and dead dog!"

Longarm decided, "*Bueno,* that *is* the corner they found that cry for help in, and your hounds ain't sniffing in any other corners. Do you reckon they could track her out of that corner towards a more recent place she might have been?"

Perrita hunkered down and talked to her *sabuesos* in Coahuiltecan. Brujo just looked befuddled. Bruja ran her wet nose along the wall to the front door and sat down, panting.

Perrita said, "She tells me that Tejana was brought in through that door and left the same way. They did not give her time for to piss. I don't see why they bothered for to stop here."

Longarm said, "They swapped ponies. Ain't no ponies out back right now. Could your hounds tell us whether that palomino I'm riding came from here to begin with?"

The bloodhounds could and did. Perrita let them sniff at droppings from the fresh pony Longarm had won at gunpoint, and talked them out of backtracking it by leading it around to the corral out back. This time it was Brujo who sniffed along the trampled earth near the water trough and sat down to bay at the stars, sounding sort of smug.

Longarm was starting to pick up their lingo. He nodded and said, "Those killers helped themselves to fresh mounts before they left and turned their own stock loose, along with any other ponies in this corral, to run off and fend for themselves, leaving trails of their own to follow. It's an old horse-raiding trick, used by red and white horse thieves because it works so well."

He strode over to the gaping kitchen door and fetched a couple of buckets to carry to the yard pump as Perrita asked what happened next.

Longarm began pumping as he told her, "First I wet down that grave in hopes of them poor souls keeping till they can be dug up to be buried right. Then I figured, seeing it's still early and the sky is clear, we'd ride on to the next *posada* along this road to the west. I'd hate to be here when, not if, the next *rurale* patrol comes along, and after that, nobody here can tell us whether they noticed which way some desperados might have lit out with a redhead, or which way we head to find that Escondijo Yaqui."

Perrita protested, "Is no Yaqui in Serranias del Burro. The Indios on this side are my people. The Indios on the other side speak another tongue but, like us, are now Cristianos living much the same as our Hispano neighbors. Yaqui speak the same tongue as the Chihuahua you will find on the other side of the mountains, but you will find no Yaqui this far east."

Longarm asked about Apache. She made the sign of the cross and replied, *"Sí, in Los Burros* perhaps Apache, with no Yaqui. I am not certain whether this is any better. Either pagan *raza* would be as likely to kill you slowly and rape me *muy mucho*. How do you know those *robares de la mujer Americana* did not, how you say, back their tracks? They say El Pico's stronghold is among the *jacales* in the poor parts of Ciudad Acuña. For why would he be holding that woman somewhere nobody has ever heard of, so far from his base, eh?"

Longarm started to say it made no sense for kidnappers to carry a victim half a hard day's ride out of town if they meant to keep her there in town. But then he recalled what those killers he'd just met up with had pulled with the riding stock and decided, "You could be on to something. Nobody else was able to cut that redhead's trail after she'd been seen here and scribbled that one short message. So it well may be they flimflammed her by telling her they were taking her to a hideout that don't exist, knowing she'd want us to know, and *giving her the chance* to leave that message as a red herring."

Perrita eagerly finished for him, "*Sí,* then they simply took her back to Ciudad Acuña for to lock her up right in town, if she is still alive! We could easily make it back to

Ciudad Acuña by dawn if we left right now."

Longarm said, "I know. And then we'd still be wondering where in tarnation they might be holding Fiona Palmer. So we'd best press on at least as far as the Burros. We won't know for certain they never took her on to that Yaqui hideout until we ask other folks whether they can recall such unusual traveling companions or ever heard tell of any place called a Yaqui hideout over this way."

Perrita said, "I think you are not thinking this through, *querido*. We have already brushed with *hombres malos* before *reaching* your *chingado* mountains, and they say Victorio is hiding out on this side of the Rio Bravo. You will find no Escondijo Yaqui in hills infested not with any *Yaqui* but with many, all too many *Apache*! More better to ride back to Ciudad Acuña with me and perhaps we can find time for *el rapto supremo* along the way, no?"

To which Longarm could only reply, "No. I got to check out what I got to check out. All I'm sure of is that a redhead seen here wrote on that very wall she was being taken to Escondijo Yaqui, not to Ciudad Acuña or anywhere else."

Perrita stared sullenly down at the pump between them as she shook her head and said, "*Maldito,* nobody told me my *sabuesos* and me were to die for this *gringa* we never met. They never told us we would be asked to follow you *this* far out of town! I like you, Custis. You know how much I like to rage with you lying down. But do not ask me to go on with anybody into Apacheria after dark!"

So he said he followed her drift, and got out a gold double eagle and some silver cartwheels to go with the loot she'd salvaged back at the scene of that gunfight. She took the *dinero,* but bit her lip and looked as if she was fixing to cry as she protested, "Is too much for the services of Bruja and Bruja. I hope you do not think I am the sort of *mujer* one has to pay for *other* services!"

He said, "Perish the thought. I'm too romantic-natured to pay for my slap and tickle." He started pumping water as he added, "If you mean to go you'd best get going. You got a long night's ride ahead of you."

She sobbed, "Now I have made you *irritado*. I do not wish for you to hate me. *Te adoro y llevo mi corozón*. Is just that I am too young for to die, and you are most certain to be killed if you push on into those wild mountains with Victorio almost anywhere south of the Rio Bravo and those mountains infested with our *own* Apaches in *quieter* times!"

Longarm finished filling the first bucket, and commenced to fill the second as he he asked her one last favor. When she started to shuck her blouse, he said, "If you're going I'd like you to just walk off without looking back. I hate long good-byes and we've both had our say. So go with God and let's say no more about it."

He bent to pick up both buckets. When he turned he was alone in the dark yard. He toted the water inside to pour it slowly over the clay clods of the mass grave, hoping to sort of pickle the murdered family for now. As he came in with his second load of water, he could smell something good cooking in the kitchen. The Mexican hot tamale had been an Indian invention when you studied on it, and that bar up front was well stocked too.

But when he sloshed the last of three trips for water over the soggy clay and ambled into the kitchen, he found nothing there but a tempting aroma. He followed it out front to find a heaping tray of tamales, tapas, and frijoles waiting for him on the end of the bar along with a side order of tortillas, a glass of *pulque*, and that chemise Fiona Palmer had worn.

The front door gaped open to the starry night.

Hoping she'd just gone out to move their riding stock around to the back, Longarm ambled outside to see his fresh palomino where he'd left it tethered and ready to ride on. Perrita, her mule, and those two bloodhounds were gone. He cocked his head, and could just make out the already distant sound of hoofbeats.

He smiled thinly and declared aloud, "Well, you can't win 'em all. But damn it, I needed those dogs, and her ass wasn't bad either!"

Then he went back inside to turn that tepid glass of *pulque* into a sort of Mexican boilermaker, with a shot of tequila from the back bar. He considered hanging on to the tequila, but decided he'd better not. Drinking alone was like jacking off alone when it came to the pleasure, and could get you in a lot more trouble when it came to bad habits.

He hadn't realized how hungry he was until he dug into the supper she'd prepared for him as a parting gift. He ate it standing up, to unkink his legs for the night riding he faced. A man riding a strange trail in the dark tended to hug his mount tighter with his knees than usual. Ponies could see pretty well in all but total darkness, and when they couldn't see they wouldn't take another step. But a rider who couldn't see where his mount knew the way was still inclined to ride sort of tight.

He forced himself to top the meal off with the bland tortillas, not knowing when he'd get to eat again and having learned from Mexican pals that the almost tasteless pancake-shaped tortillas made of white corn flour blanched with quicklime were the true staff of life south of, say, the Arkansas River. Tortillas took forever to digest, and in the meantime kept the spicier Mexican grub tamped down, so you didn't get hungry again as soon as you might have trying to exist on hot tamales alone.

He tore a page from his notebook to leave a message on the bar for the next lawmen who might show up. He held it down with the now-empty *pulque* glass, gathered up that chemise, and carried it out front to store in a saddlebag as he told the palomino, "You've had your beauty rest. Now I aim to take you around to the back and put some water and cracked corn in you before we ride on."

The pony was in no position to argue. So within the hour—it was now getting on towards ten P.M.—they were wending westward towards the looming black unknown of the Serrianas del Burro. They followed the same coach road because there was no other logical path to follow. He didn't know what lay ahead, but coach roads hardly ever led over the edge of a cliff.

This seemed to go on for a million years as Longarm cursed Perrita and himself in turn. Fair was fair and if she was being a sissy, she was still more of an authority on Mexico than he was and he could be on a wild-goose chase into mighty rough parts.

So he was relieved a good two hours later when he spied a pinpoint of light against the blackness and decided that had to be the next former coach stop cum *posada* along the no-longer-in-use mail and passenger route. The Mexican postal service had given up on mail through such natural bandit country in favor of a more southern route *los rurales* found easier to police.

Since travelers in a hurry still followed the shorter if riskier way through the Burros, there still stood a *posada* every few hours' ride, and as he rode closer Longarm could see that was what he was riding toward. It said so, in blue letters painted along the 'dobe over the open front entrance, lit up by a hanging lantern. So he dismounted, tethered the palomino out front, and strode in to the sounds of guitar and castanets.

The gal in the flamenco skirt dancing in the center of the taproom stopped clicking her castanets and froze in an interesting pose as the guitar stopped strumming and a whole room full of Mexicans stared at Longarm poker-faced.

He nodded and went over to the bar, looking neither to the right nor left as he ordered *cerveza*. But naturally, a burly Mexican lounging against the bar in a gilded straw sombrero, and with two Colt '73's worn low and tied down, asked Longarm sullenly, "Hey, gringo, for why are you staring at me?"

Chapter 14

Longarm knew he was supposed to say he hadn't been looking at anybody so the bully could ask who he'd just called a liar. Longarm turned to lock eyes with the big Mexican, smiled pleasantly, and replied, "I was looking at you because I thought you were somebody I know. But I see I was wrong. This other *caballero* wore the same sort of sombrero, but he had a brain under it."

The local hero stepped away from the bar, eyes narrowed but smiling back, as he softly asked, "Is that the buzzing of an annoying mosquito I just heard, or did somebody just imply I was *estupido*?"

Longarm pleasantly replied, "Not I. You are not my type, even if I went in for picking up *muchachos* in *cantinas,* as some people wearing the hat of a *picaflor* seem to go in for. So I have no reason to flatter a *pendejo* by calling him *estupido*."

The fat woman behind the bar slid Longarm's mug of draft across the waxed oak to him, flatly stating, "*Bueno,* you are both so brave I am about to wet myself. *Pero la vida es breve* when you don't throw fifty or sixty years away *por nada*! So behave yourselves or take it outside, *muchachos*. I am trying for to run a respectable place here, and we just mopped the floor tiles."

The bully in the gilded hat protested, "*Esa condenado me frego bien!*" But the fat *pasadera* replied, "No, he didn't, Gordo. You started it, and I have asked you before not to play that *tu madre* game in here."

Longarm volunteered, "Gordo and me were just *familiardad, mi patrona*. I feel sure he would like a *cerveza* on me. Isn't that so, Gordo?"

The burly bully looked confused as he managed, "Only if there is no argument about who buys the next round, *cabron*!"

Since *cabron* only meant to imply your wife was cheating on you and everyone knew it, and since Longarm didn't have a wife, he let that pass. The game was called *tu madre,* or "you mother," because it called for some serious action at the point where total strangers mentioned mothers or any other female relations they had never been properly introduced to.

As Gordo got his own suds, which might well have been the point of his veiled attack, he grudgingly raised his mug to say, "*Salud y chingate, extranjero*. For how did you get to have such a mouth in a world filled with sensitive souls such as I?"

Longarm snorted, "*No me jodas*. You just heard me smooth things over. Do you want to get us both thrown out?"

Gordo shrugged and decided, "Later perhaps. Where have you come from and where are you riding, my smooth-talking one?"

The guitar and castanets had started up behind him again as Longarm replied truthfully that he'd just come from Ciudad Acuña but wasn't sure just where he was headed. He explained, "Some friends asked me to meet them at some place called Escondijo Yaqui. Nobody I have asked, so far, seems to know where it is."

Gordo laughed harshly and called out, "Listen to this *pendejo*! He says he wishes for to ride to a place called Escondijo Yaqui!"

So some of the others laughed too, and when Longarm asked what he was missing, Gordo said, "Your sense of hearing. Is no such place as Escondijo Yaqui, *cabron.* Thanks for the *cerveza. Tengo que mear como el demonio.*"

So while Gordo went off to piss like the devil, Longarm asked the fat old gal behind the bar about Escondijo Yaqui. She shrugged her massive shoulders and allowed she'd never heard of such a place.

Longarm finished his suds, leaving his change on the bar as he debated with himself whether to get the hell out of such unfriendly surroudings or try to make friends with at least one local who knew what Gordo and those others had been laughing about.

The music stopped and the dancing gal stopped clicking castanets and stomping the tiles with her high heels. Longarm was only mildly surprised when she seemed to be joining him at the bar. It seemed to go with being taken for a rich gringo down this way. The real surprise was when she opened her mouth to twang in perfect English, or what sounded like Dixie leastways, "You'd best get out of here right now, country boy! That Gordo is a mean one, and as he passed us he said something about cleaning your plow for you, by starlight on the trail."

Longarm signaled the *posadera* to serve the dancing gal as he sized her up. On second glance, she had blue eyes to go with her black hair. And her cameo features, which could be taken for Castilian at first glance, could just as easily be that mixture of Scotch-Irish and Cherokee the folks back in West-by-God-Virginia called "mountain white."

As the *posadera* poured she quietly murmured, "We do not allow *that* sort of disorderly conduct at this *posada* either, Señorita."

The oddly misplaced Anglo gal in Mexican costume calmly replied in good Spanish that no gal willing to sell her ass would dance that hard for centavos tossed at her feet. So the *posadera* just warned them not to even think about renting a room for the night, and moved off to let them work it out.

Longarm introduced himself by name, leaving out the outfit he rode for and what he was doing south of the border. She said he could call her Geneva and that last names didn't matter. So he allowed he would, and added, "I don't see how old Gordo could be laying for me on my way to this Escondijo Yaqui, because I don't know where it is and everyone I ask keeps telling me there's no such place!"

Geneva laughed wildly and said, "You big silly! It ain't Escondijo *Yaqui* you'd be looking for, it's Escondijo *Yanqui,* the Yankee Hideout as the durned Mexicans call it, but bite your tongue when you get up yonder because the folks hiding out there are pure old unreconstructed Rebels who rid down here to hide out when Lee and Jeff Davis lost their nerve back in '65!"

Longarm laughed and said, "Well, I never!" But of course he'd heard of other Confederate holdouts resettled as far off as Brazil after the war. Some had just been stubborn, like those New England Tories who'd headed for Canada after their side had lost the American Revolution. Others had likely lit out because they'd been wanted for such crimes as mistreating Union prisoners or murdering suddenly disobedient slaves, black soldiers in Army blue, or other white Southerners who hadn't seemed as enthusiastic about the Lost Cause towards the end.

Geneva leaned closer lest they be overheard as she told him, "You want to ride south a ways and swing wide because Gordo and his pals will be expecting you to ride due north from here."

He said, "That road out front don't run north or south, Miss Geneva. It carried me this far east to west."

She nodded and replied, "Why did you think they called it a hideout? These foothill hogbacks and hollers run southeast to northwest where you see a beaten path or not. You want to get safely south a few miles and cut east to the first holler. It ain't the right one. But do you follow it northwest until sunrise, you'll be way north of Gordo and his pals when you cut west, over hills and dale, to follow the second holler west of here towards the unmapped badlands of that Big Bend country of Texas. That north end of the Burros is laid out much the same. With secluded green hollers surrounded by jaggedy rimrocks to discourage a buzzard from settling."

Longarm nodded soberly and said, "Sounds like parts of the Four Corners country to the north I've ridden through. You'll get those hidden settlements of Indians, Mormons, or worse off in the middle of what's nothing but nothing much on the survey maps. Have you ever been to this Escondijo Yanqui, Miss Geneva?"

The oddly misplaced Dixie belle hesitated, nodded, and confessed, "I ran away from there when I was sixteen. I barely recall the home in Alabam' we left when the bluebellies came, looking to arrest both my big brothers. We lit out for Texas, and when they kept after us we moved down here with other wanted Rebs. So I was *raised* in and about what the Mexicans call Escondijo Yanqui. We always called it Esperanza Nuevo, meaning new hope. When I was sixteen I thought it was the most tedious little settlement on God's green earth."

She drained her mug and set it aside as she softly added, "Since then I've seen other parts, and be it ever so humble . . ."

"You can't go back?" Longarm gently asked, hoping like hell she was as homesick as she sounded.

Geneva shook her head and quietly replied, "My leaving was ugly. My daddy had died and my mamma and older brothers couldn't manage me when I took it in my fool head I loved a dago."

"You ran off with this Mexican your family didn't approve of?" Longarm asked, trying to sound more interested then he was in a story he'd been told before more than once.

Geneva said, "They weren't down on him because he was Mex. We'd been shown to good timber, water, and grazing by Mex pals of our Texas kith and kin. We'd been granted Mex citizenship by the Juarez bunch, and who did you think we sold our stock to? You can't raise *cotton* in Esperanza Nuevo. But we do right well raising beef and fine ponies bred from Confederate cavalry mounts with some thoroughbred lineage. My family was down on Luis because he was just what they said he was, a lazy charmer with a mean streak who couldn't hold his liquor or keep his hands off anything in a skirt. I left him less than a year after I ran off with him. I came home from work, since he wouldn't work, to find him drunk as a skunk, in bed with the next-door neighbor's twelve-year-old daughter. My eldest brother had warned me Luis liked his gals younger than most grown men."

Longarm got out his pocket watch, nodded, and said, "One draw over and then two draws west. I'd best get cracking if I want to work well west of Gordo's bunch before it commences to lighten up outside. I'm sorry things turned out so poorly for you and that *hombre fregado* you left home with, Miss Geneva. I know better than to advise a lady about such family matters. So I thank you for the directions and we'll say no more about it."

He ticked his hat brim to her and quietly slipped away from the bar to leave, unopposed, as Geneva flounced across the floor to talk to her guitar player.

As he untethered the palomino he told it, "I was aiming to water and fodder you here before we moved on, old gal, but this has turned out a rougher neighborhood than a lady like you ought to hang around in. So we'll talk about watering you some more when we come to more water. Ought to be some in these foothills, after all that recent rain."

The palomino didn't argue as he led her out of earshot in the dark, mounted up, and rode off the coach road into what he hoped to be a northwest-to-southeast draw, carpeted but not choked with chaparral he trusted his mount to avoid with her keener night vision. She only dragged his boots now and again through mesquite or paloverde as she looked out mostly for her own pretty hide.

He could just make out the hogback ridge to his left against the starry sky as they worked their way south. When they came upon a deer trail cutting east through a visible gap in the hogback, Longarm opted to follow it. It led as he'd hoped to another slightly lower draw, or holler as that Dixie gal had called it, so Longarm reined his mount northwest to follow it as, somewhere in the night, a hoot owl explained why they called this sort of travel a ride along the owlhoot trail.

Horses saw better by starlight, and Longarm didn't have those bloodhounds now that he could really use them. But he'd learned to scout sharp at night against men red and white who'd been out to kill him. So when he heard a faint jingle up ahead, he reined in to smoothly dismount and hold the palomino on short rein with his free hand over her muzzle, letting her breathe as long as she didn't inhale deep enough for a whinny. Men, and horses, had learned long ago that a man of modest size could cut off a horse's wind by covering just its nostrils, no horse being able to breathe through its toothy mouth.

As he stood there, telling his own heart not to thump so damned loud, he heard a soft voice call out, "*Quien es?* Custis, is that you trying to scare a girl half to death?"

To which he could only reply, "Speak for yourself, Miss Geneva. For a minute I had you down as one of them *chindi* spirits the Apache tell of. What can I do for you, ma'am?"

She called out, "Take me with you. You'll never find the place alone and I've been thinking about what you said, ever since you said there was no point in saying anything to me about going home."

Longarm led the palomino afoot to where the Dixie belle from the *posada* sat a dapple gray sidesaddle, in a more sedate dark skirt with a bolero jacket on over her low-cut blouse. He saw she'd put on a flat-topped Spanish sombrero as he mounted up beside her and softly pointed out, "I never offered you any advice at all, Miss Geneva."

She said, "That's likely why it sank in so deep. I've been given the same advice by ladies and gents or friendly whores and gamblers I've met up with in many a tacky cantina where I was dancing for loose change because I just can't forget my tight uprbringing. I don't know how many times I've told others it was no use. How there was no way I could ever go home because I'd have to admit I'd been wrong and that I should have listened to my own loving kin."

Longarm didn't know whether she could see his nod as he soberly told her, "You were right, ma'am. There's no way on earth you could ever go back without admitting you'd been a headstrong brat of not-too-sweet sixteen. How much they'd low-rate such a prodigal daughter would most likely depend on just how loving her own kin really were."

She sobbed, "I know my momma loves me. For I've never stopped loving her and I want to go home now, Custis. So will you carry me on home?"

To which he could only reply, "I'd be proud to, Miss Generva, but you're going to have to lead the way. For I have no idea where we're headed or why some Mexican kidnappers were headed there with another young lady entirely!"

Chapter 15

Geneva had been right about one thing. Longarm would have had one hell of a time fiding the place if he hadn't been riding with a gal raised in those hills. Sunrise caught them threading through jagged-ass bare crags that all looked alike, and Geneva agreed with Perrita about the danger of Apaches.

So they holed up for the day in a box canyon she'd camped in once before while running away from home. It was an ideal hideout for bad Indian country. Since it was a box canyon, there was only one way in or out between nearly vertical cliffs. Camping where there was no other way out was a situation to be avoided by Indians hunted for sport by *los federales* with field guns. Moreover, there was enough grazing for two ponies and enough brushwood for a few modest campfires, but not nearly enough for your average Indian band of thirty braves with their dependents.

Thanks to that recent rain, there was a trickle of running water along the wash carved a tad lower than the rest of the canyon bed. A rock slide had dammed one stretch to form a natural swimming hole full of fairy shrimp and the tiny tadpoles of spadefoot toads. But when she suggested a cool-off dip after all that riding, Longarm told her to go ahead while he made camp under an overhang a ways upstream. Aside from the fact that she'd likely gone swimming in the nude there with her no-good sweetheart, any man who'd do the same with a good-looking gal he was escorting home to at least two big brothers would have to be a total asshole.

So he hobbled their riding stock on green sedge alongside the water further up, and lugged their two saddles up some scree to a ledge under that overhang, where they'd be shaded all day if they stayed that long. Geneva's sidesaddle was laden with more possibles than his McClellan. He'd already learned she'd been vagabonding all over Mexico on her own since she'd left that Luis and a few other no-goods after him. She'd said she'd learned to ride alone, picking up some local musicians to strum flamenco guitar music behind her whenever she found a place to dance for her supper and maybe a little traveling money. She'd said that that guitar-strummer back where they'd met, a kid called Ramon, had been sore as hell when she'd allowed she was cutting out on him and he could keep that night's take. Old Ramon had doubtless been hoping for a few more nights with her, and more than some pocket jingle. Young gents could get to hoping as they strummed away behind the clicking heels and swirling skirts of a flamenco dancer. For such dancing was designed to get one's hopes up.

But Longarm spread their separate bedrolls within easy talking but not touching distance atop beds of tule reed he'd cut down along the narrow floodplain of that seasonal rivulet. It hadn't been easy to ignore the distant but plainly visible naked lady splashing in that all-too-shallow pool downstream. He'd thought she was built mighty nice in her dancing outfit. He could see how Ramon could have been so sore about her hauling ass. Longarm knew he wasn't supposed to want her ass, and it was starting to hurt like hell.

You didn't cook over fire far from other whites in Apacheria. If it was tougher to spot a distant flame by daylight, rising smoke could be seen for miles. So he'd opened some more cans of pork and beans, with one dessert of tomato preserves to share, by the time the clean-smelling gal in just her sweaty blouse and skirt joined him, with her bolero and sombrero in her hands.

She tossed them on her laid-out bedroll and sank down beside him on his, saying, "That's the first real bath I've had in days. It's easy to forget you could use a bath, surrounded by poor people in a dry climate. What happens next?"

He handed her a can of pork and beans with the spoon from his mess kit, saying, "Next we take turns on watch and see if we can catch a few good winks. Then we ride on by starlight, and you did figure it as two nights in the saddle, didn't you?"

She dug in as she nodded and replied, "We'll want to ride in after sunrise. Some of the unreconstructed Rebels of Esperanza Nuevo are mighty proddy, and even the womenfolk go armed away from their own dooryards. How are you to eat your own breakfast without this spoon?"

Longarm said, "It saves time to just sort of drink from the can. I learned rougher table manners than my poor old momma approved of once I took to camping with the cavalry."

She brightened and asked, "Were you in the War Between the States? You seem about the same age as my younger big brother, and he rode with Bedford Forrest against Fort Pillow!"

Longarm allowed he disremembered who he'd ridden with or half the things he'd done since he'd run off to play soldier with the other kids in a war that never should have happened. She'd as much as told him why her Rebel kinsmen had fled the States during Reconstruction. The massacre of those colored Union troops at Fort Pillow had seemed cowardly and disgusting even to many a Confederate officer at the time.

Nobody who'd led Rebel charges at Shiloh and Chickamauga could be called a coward, but General N. B. Forrest had been an uneducated and poorly brought-up natural killer who'd lived through the war to help found the K.K.K. and die peacefully in bed as the president of a postwar railroad back in '77. Not knowing what this proved, Longarm made no comments on her brother's military service as they put away their canned breakfast.

He told her to see if she could get some sleep while he stood the first watch. She allowed she was still too wound up, between the tense situation back at that *posada* and the thought of being almost home after all those wasted years.

She said, "I suppose I ought to thank your friend Gordo if ever I see him again. Had not he had it in for you, there's no saying how things might have turned out back yonder. But I know I'd have never screwed up the gumption to go home at last if you hadn't needed me to guide you to Esperanza Nuevo."

Longarm swallowed and said, "Yes, you would have. I read about this doctor over in Vienna Town who's studied on the way our brains play tricks on us. With all of Old Mexico to wander, what do you reckon made you drift to that out-of-the-way *posada* less than a hundred miles from home? That unconscious mind those alienists write about was leading you home like a long-lost pigeon, Miss Geneva."

She protested, "That's silly. If I had any hankering for these parts, it was only because it's less like Mexico than some other parts of Mexico and, oh, Custis, I'm so durned sick of Mexico!"

When he just swallowed more beans, she explained. "The country has some pretty scenery and lots of the people are nice. But it ain't my scenery and they ain't my people and the government down here is bad as the tyranny of the Damnyankee!"

Longarm said, "Worse. President Hayes ended the last pesky rules of the Reconstruction when he got elected. He was a Union war hero, so he could get away with that. The States of the Old South are all run by Southerners these days, and they've even reconstituted the Texas Rangers in spite of Chickamauga. So to tell the pure truth, there's no pressing need for you or any of your kith and kin to live down here under the Diaz dictatorship."

She stared off down the canyon as she murmured, "They said something about my big brothers being war criminals just before we lit out from Alabam'."

Longarm shrugged, slurped some tomato preserves to cut the greasy aftertaste of pork and beans, and handed her the can as he told her, "They talked about hanging Jeff Davis, but they never did. The only Rebel war criminals I recall being hung, aside from the bunch mixed up in the killing of Abe Lincoln, was that Major Wirz who'd commanded that Confederate prison camp at Andersonville in Georgia. If they allowed N. B. Forrest to die in bed, I doubt they'd still be after either of your big brothers, Miss Geneva."

She brightened and declared, "It's worth writing to find out! I'll tell them what you said as soon as we get there!"

Then she polished off the last of the tomato preserves, and allowed she was commencing to feel sleepy after all. So she wriggled into her bedroll, and Longarm could tell by more wriggles she was taking off her duds to sleep naked under the covers. So he lit a cheroot and told his fool pecker that was no business of their own as it still went on twitching, blast its willful nature.

But by his second or third spaced-out smoke he was having way more trouble staying awake than he was having with his old organ-grinder. Thanks to that earlier day-camping with Perrita, he'd had more sex than he'd needed and not enough sleep getting this far out of Ciudad Acuña, and the farther he rode the more he suspected Perrita could have been right about this being a wild-goose chase into dangerous territory.

Geneva had described the so-called Yankee hideout as a community of around thirty Rebel families clustered around an adobe Baptist church in a fertile but secluded valley with raw rimrock all around where the Burro Mountains came down to the border a few miles on. The parts of Texas across the brawling Rio Bravo were no improvement and just as unsettled. The badlands of the Big Bend country were infested with bad men, red and white, but unsettled by decent folks of any complexion because it was mortally hard to wrest an honest living from imposing cliffs and windswept barren crags, with no wagon traces worth mentioning.

He supressed a yawn, and tried to inspire some alertness thinking about that *pendejo* Gordo and his pals. But they didn't merit much thinking, now that Geneva had shown him how to circle them wide in the dark. Speculating on the motives of saloon fighters such as Gordo was a waste of brain sweat. His kind, Anglo or Mexican, lived for showing everyone how tough they could talk. The notion of helping themselves to a stranger's boots, cash, guns, and pony had likely entered into it as well. But Longarm doubted he'd ever lay eyes on that gilded straw sombrero or its fat-ass owner again, and so the question before the house was what those other Mexican gunslicks had had in mind when they'd told a captive redhead they were carrying her to a place she'd understood to be Escondijo *Yaqui* instead of *Yanqui*. It made no more sense as a hideout for Mexican kidnappers by either name. Perrita's notion that the redhead had been told a big fib, allowed to scrawl that message as a red herring, and been backtracked to the slums of that border town, got much easier to buy as a gal from Escondijo Yanqui sold him an ever clearer image of an Anglo-Saxon enclave disgusted with the current Mexican government and wary of any strangers.

After Geneva had slept over four hours and had commenced to stir in her sleep, as hipbones on hard bedding inspired one to stir, he moved over to gently shake her, and when she stretched like a kitten and smiled up at him with both bare arms above her head and her bare breasts peeking over the horizon of her top blanket like a pair of rising moons, Longarm said, "I got my eyelids propped open with toothpicks and it's commencing to hurt. Do you feel up to a turn on watch?"

She began to wriggle into her duds under the covers as she allowed she'd been dreaming of home, and asked what she was supposed to watch out for.

He said, "You never know. It's going on noon and nothing but those grazing ponies down by the creek have stirred for hours. That's how come I want you to stand watch. Things happen when you're least expecting them to. That's how come they call 'em surprises. I'll leave this Winchester and some more cans here at the foot of your bedroll whilst I climb into mine for a spell."

He got out his pocket watch and placed it on her bedding beside the stock of his Winchester, adding, "Here, wake me up in, say, four hours unless something happens sooner."

She said she would as she went on dressing under her covers. Longarm waited until he saw she was sincerely up, and then he shucked his boots and took off his gun rig to coil it up in the crown of his inverted coffee-brown Stetson before he slid into his own roll wearing shirt and jeans to just let go for a spell.

But the next thing Longarm knew he seemed to be stark naked in the Denver Public Library, only nobody seemed to notice as he tried to take a big book from a shelf to cover his raging erection before the pretty librarian, Miss Morgana Floyd of the Arvada Orphan Asylum, noticed how silly he looked.

As she rose from her desk and came over to tell him he had to let her stamp that book if he wanted to take it home, Longarm stammered, "I was fixing to read it here, Miss Morgana, and when did they put you in charge of this library? Ain't you supposed to be riding herd on all those orphans off to the west of town?"

The petite brunette, who somehow reminded him of this flamenco dancer down Mexico way, said, "Oh, for heaven's sake, Custis, hand me that book. It's not as if I've never seen you with a hard-on before!"

Then she was whispering something as she shook him by the shoulder, and he woke up to see it really was that flamenco dancer from down Mexico way.

Geneva whispered, "Don't go back to sleep again. Someone's coming!"

Longarm sat bolt upright, fully awake, as off in the distance he too heard three or more male voices harmonizing, or trying to harmonize, as they sang more or less, about their fool *carazónes*. It was as tough for a Mexican songwriter to leave out *carazón* as it was for Stephen Foster to leave out darkies. It was likely a great temptation to use something that had rhymed the last time.

Longarm was out from under the covers and into his boots and gun by the time they could make out the golden glint of sunlight bouncing off a gilded straw sombrero.

Geneva gasped, "It's Gordo and his bunch! But why did they trail us this far? I didn't think they were *that* sore at you, Custis!"

He quietly asked, "Wasn't that Ramon, strumming guitar for you at that *posada,* sporting a purple satin shirt?"

When she said that sounded like Ramon, Longarm moved over to get the Winchester on her bedding as he soberly replied, "There's your answer then. You *said* old Ramon was sore as hell at you for lighting out with me, and Gordo never liked me to begin with. So they've joined forces, knowing where you and me were headed, and knowing they'd have us all to themselves in these mighty uninhabited hills!"

Chapter 16

The noonday sun flashed off the swishing white tail of a palomino almost as well as if it had been gilded straw. So Gordo spotted the ponies way upstream before one of his pals yelled, *"Mire!"* as white woodsmoke rose against the red rocks enclosing that end of the box canyon. Gordo reined in with a grim chortle to declare, "I told you all was only one *entrada*. Now see what the *chi chi cabron* has done out here in Apacheria! Has lit a fire for to have tea in the Anglo manner with your *puta,* Ramon. Let us leave our mounts here and move in on foot as we join them, eh?"

As Gordo, his two pals, and the pissed-off musician Ramon dismounted and began to tether their ponies in a clump of *chamisa,* the guitarist in the purple satin shirt warned, "Remember what we agreed on about that *chiflada,* Geneva. I wish for to have her at least once while she is still alive, *comprende*?"

Gordo's voice was a soft purr as he said, *"Bueno,* I have been meaning to talk to you about that money you promised us for helping you get your *perida* back. I mean no offense, my famous *flamencero,* but I have yet to see all this money you say you have for us. May we see just a little of it, *por favor,* before we move in on that gringo with the double-action gun?"

Ramon took out his bankroll and flashed it. Ramon didn't know Gordo very well. The big beefy *buscadero* struck with the speed and grace of a cornered scorpion, and then Ramon was sinking to his knees with both hands to his throat and a look of surprised horror in his eyes as blood spurted far and wide from between his fingers.

As Ramon crumpled in a bloody heap on the blood-spattered *caliche* at Gordo's feet, one of Gordo's pals sighed and said, "*Maldito,* I was looking forward to wearing that satin shirt. Was *muy linda* before you slashed his *chingado* throat!"

Gordo wiped the bloody blade of his bowie on the dark leather of the *chapaderos* worn over his cotton pants as he replied, "It could not be helped. No man rides with me dressed like a *maracon fregado,* and I did not wish that gringo up ahead for to hear any shots. Pick up that roll he dropped and hand it to me. We are wasting time talking about suckers of cock in purple shirts!"

As he put his bowie away and drew both six-guns, nobody argued. Gordo was not a man to argue with. But as they eased up the canyon, three abreast, the one who'd handed Gordo the money mildly observed, "He may have dressed *de la izquierda,* but he was *loco* for to get that *mujer* back, no?"

Gordo shrugged and decided, "Strumming his guitar while she danced was as much work as he felt capable of, the soft-handed *mariposa.* I said we have spoken enough about him. Is that big gringo with double-action and a big mouth I am interested in now!"

He waved a gun muzzle at the canyon wall to his right as he went on. "We want to get as close as we can before they see us. Follow me in *enfila singular* and let us see how far we can move through that *alameda* growing at the base of the cliffs, eh?"

Having been trained in military scouting as a kid, Longarm had expected anyone with a lick of sense to do just that. So he'd sent Geneva up to the head of the canyon with a box of matches and some hastily gathered tinder, while he'd worked his own way along tangled crack willow and cottonwood along the well-watered bases of the canyon walls. So when Gordo led his two pals single file into the same *alameda,* Longarm was not only there but to their rear as they flattened out against the red rock to sneak toward the smudge fire Geneva had lit as bait beyond the hobbled ponies.

Longarm had seen what they'd just done to another Mexican who'd trusted them. So he knew none of them would hesitate to backshoot him if the tables were turned. But he'd still been brought up by decent folks. So even as he raised his cocked and loaded saddle gun, he still found himself calling out, *"Manos arriba! Estoy sincero."*

But Gordo whirled to scream, *"Chingate! Tey voy a mandar pa'l carajo!"* as he swung both guns up to blaze away at Longarm through both his pals as Longarm blazed back, with grim results indeed for all three Mexicans!

The two in the middle caught most of the hot flying lead, but as they went down Gordo had about emptied his wheels into them in Longarm's direction, while Longarm still had five rounds in the tube of his Winchester for Gordo to keep and cherish with his bulky torso.

It took all five to drop the big *buscadero,* and he was still saying mean things about somebody's mother as Longarm moved in with his empty Winchester and loaded six-gun.

Longarm heard Geneva's distant wail and called back, "We won. But douse that fire lest we have more company!"

Then he hunkered over the bulky form of Gordo with the Winchester across his knees and the six-gun ready for anything as he quietly asked what all the fuss had been about.

Gordo sighed and said, "You showed no respect for me. I had to make you show respect or die!"

Longarm holstered his side arm and began to reload his saddle gun as he replied, "I respect most everyone I meet until they convince this child of their stupidity. You just convinced me, Gordo. You have *fear* confounded with *respect,* and they don't even start with the same letter."

Gordo didn't answer. Longarm reached out with his free hand to feel for a pulse. That was his second mistake, and almost his last. Gordo's bowie slashed through the space a slower man's throat might have occupied as Longarm rocked back on his heels to grab the dying man's massive wrist and marvel, "Jesus H. Christ, you really *are* a dedicated son of a *maniatica*!"

To which Gordo replied by coughing up blood, trying to spit it in Longarm's face, and dying with a bitter laugh when he saw he'd missed.

So Longarm let go, and finished thumbing rounds of .44-40 into the tube of his Winchester before he went through the dead man's pockets for that roll of ten-peso notes and about fifty dollars worth of gold and silver coins. He was searching the last of them when Geneva came along the canyon wall to join him, staring down in horror at the carnage in the dappled shade of the *alameda.*

She said, "I put that little fire out and covered the coals with sand. I guess we should be safe now. Are all of them really dead?"

Longarm straightned up, his Winchester muzzle aimed at the ground, to reply, "They are and you don't *guess* about how safe you might be in Apacheria. You make dead certain, unless you cnjoy being dead. So we'll gather the rest of our loot and be on our way, Miss Geneva."

She didn't understand what he meant about loot until she was helping him stuff the saddlebags of the four surviving ponies with guns, silver-mounted gunbelts, spurs, silver conchas worth at least four bits apiece, and so on.

When he asked, she agreed that her Rebel kith and kin up in Esperanza Nuevo had to trade for such goods at a steep price with the outside world, mostly with *ciboleros,* as most Mexicans called the halfbreed traders who'd been better known as Comancheros on the Staked Plains when they still traded "no questions" with Quill Indians who could always use a gun or a bottle of firewater and had plenty of horses to spare.

As they broke camp and mounted up to lead the four extra ponies on a long lead fashioned from Gordo's reata, Longarm explained he wanted her to have the extra cash, but said, "I want you to introduce me as a no-questions trader you met on your way home, with Victorio on the prowl. I need an excuse to ask some questions without having to offer too many answers about current conditions up in the States. I just hate to argue politics or religion with folks set in their ways, and I'd say anyone hiding out from a Reconstruction that's over and done with is sort of set, no offense."

As he reached across the gap between their stirrups with the feed sack he'd filled with the money from four dead men, Geneva hesitated and protested, "I can't take money off a man I've been traveling with unescorted! Whatever might people think?"

He jingled the sack, saying, "They'll think you made out fairly well as a flamenco dancer. Anyone who wants to accuse you of being a soiled dove is going to do so whether you come home flush or broke. So you may as well come home flush, and there ain't nearly enough here to pay you for all those wasted years on the lonesome vagabond trail."

So she took the sack from him with a sob, and turned her face away to say something about her momma telling her something.

They rode on for well over an hour before Geneva, in the lead, reined in to point at what looked like just another hogback of red rock aimed upslope to the southwest and exclaimed, "We're closer to home than I thought! There's a rock shelter on the far side of that big slab of sandstone. Wandering Apache would never suspect it was there."

But Longarm shook his head and pointed out, "Victorio and his band ain't the only Na-déné speakers we got to worry about in this neck of Apacheria, Miss Geneva. They call this high country all the way out to Tombstone Apacheria because you meet up with the ones like Victorio most anywhere they wander. But when they ain't wandering, the so-called Apache hole up in semi-permanent mountain *rancheritas*. So a good many of the Indians who might have spotted that smoke we had to send up will know this country as well as you or anyone else who's been raised in it. I reckon we'd be better off riding on now."

"In broad daylight in Apache country?" she gasped.

Longarm answered simply, "Can't be helped. The fat's in the fire, and six ponies leave a trail it don't take Indian eyes to follow. If any move in on that canyon we left, they'll cut the tracks of half a dozen shod ponies, leading in and out. Once natural-born deer hunters are on your trail, you don't hole up and wait for them to catch up to you. You keep going, riding through as many likely ambush spots as you can manage."

As he took the lead with his reloaded Winchester across his thighs, Geneva asked why on earth he'd want to ride them into likely ambush spots.

He explained. "The odds on ambush are with the ones in the lead. The ones trailing six sets of hoofprints, not knowing how many riders there might be, armed with what, are likely to slow down and do some careful scouting every time they spot a likely ambush out ahead of them. It's a trick I was taught in my misspent youth by a kindly old cavalry scout. It always works, even when the ones doing the trailing know it. *I* wouldn't want to ride fast and blind into a possible ambush. Would *you*?"

She clapped her hands and allowed with a sudden smile that she'd followed his drift. He wasn't surprised. Most military tactics were simple to grasp as soon as they were explained to a new recruit. That was how armies turned farm boys and ribbon clerks into soldiers in six weeks, if the farm boys and ribbon clerks were lucky. Longarm still felt sorry for that replacement on the line with him at Shiloh who hadn't known how to load a rifled musket. It must have felt dumb to die with an empty weapon in one hand and a ramrod in the other.

He told his new cavalry recruit, "We'll ride as fast and as far as we can manage by day, and catch some rest after sundown. The riders we call Apache don't like to ride in the gloaming. They ain't afraid of starlight as their Navaho cousins, but they believe in evil spirits called *chindi* you meet up with at twilight, when things are tougher for our eyes to decide about one way or the other. A *chindi* can change its shape to look like a stray pony, a harmless coyote, or even another human being. Lots of times the *chindi*'s feet are on backwards or its face is upside down, but who's to tell for certain in the tricky light of gloaming? So it's best not to meet anything or anybody at twilight time, lest it turn out to be a *chindi,* see?"

She said, "I reckon. What do the Apache say this twilight haunt is likely to do to them?"

Longarm soberly replied, "They can't say. Nobody who's ever met any *chindi* at twilight has ever come back to talk about it. It just *gits* you, like those wicked white children the Boogie Man carries off. The difference is, grown men and women of the Apache Nation *believe* in *chindi* and that's a break for us. We can eat our suppers in the saddle from my last cans as we just keep going. If we take a trail break from, say, the last half hour before sundown to the first half hour of total darkness, we ought to be able to catch forty winks and rest the ponies some before we push on through the night. We'll be able to ride slower by starlight because Indians can't read sign in the dark any better than the rest of us."

She asked why, in that case, they had to worry about Apache trailing them at all, once they'd made it to sundown. She said, "We could sleep a tad longer and still make it home to Esperanza Nuevo by dawn."

Longarm insisted, "That ain't the way you ride during an Indian scare. I want to make sure we have as long a lead as we can manage. Since I have done some tracking,

I'll let you in on another secret. If you know the lay of the land, once you've cut someone's trail, you don't have to follow said trail every foot of its zigzag way. Sometimes you can guess where the sly fox is headed and beeline across meadow and field to be waiting for it at its den."

She said she wished he didn't have to sound so gloomy. They rode on a spell, and then as they rested their mounts atop a rise, Longarm noticed they were heaving some and told her it was time to change mounts.

Since all six were saddled saddle-broncs, he saw no need to change his army McClellan from the spent palomino to the cinnamon gelding he'd decide on. But a lady riding sidesaddle couldn't be expected to fork her skirts over a center-fire roper. So they were both afoot and he was cinching her ladylike saddle on a fresh black mare when Geneva suddenly gasped and pointed northwest, the way they'd been heading, gasping, "Oh, my God, are those *Apache* up ahead of us?"

Longarm considered that a mighty dumb question as he soberly regarded the raggedy line of mounted men in cotton blouses, with bare legs and long black hair, staring soberly down at them from where they sat their ponies along that rise that had looked empty just a minute ago. But it wouldn't have been polite to call a lady a fool to her face. So he went on tightening her saddle cinch as he quietly replied, "Yep. I make it a party of about thirty, or a full platoon. You'd best let me do the talking, Miss Geneva. But first I'd better slip you this pocket derringer of mine. You'll know better than me how and when you'll want to use it. Don't let them see you have it until you're ready to make one last move. Then make it *sudden,* hear?"

Chapter 17

"Why don't we make a break for it?" Geneva whispered as Longarm helped her back up in her sidesaddle. She added, "We could leave the other ponies to them and try to outrun them on these fresh mounts!"

To which Longarm replied, "Run for where? None of these ponies are all that fresh, and when Horse Indians show themselves they tend to have you boxed and just want to see what you aim to do next."

She glanced back the way they'd just come. There were no riders to be seen down that way, but a whole lot of dust hung against the cloudless cobalt sky for just half a dozen ponies to have raised.

He repeated, "Let me do the talking, or signing if they don't speak Spanish like most so-called Apache. You told me earlier your kith and kin up ahead ain't had much Indian trouble since they first moved down here, and this bunch may not be with Victorio."

As he mounted the Mexican *canela* he'd chosen to lead Geneva and the other ponies on, she warned, "They'll rob us at the very least, and I'm just not up to entertaining that many gentlemen callers!"

He sighed and replied, "Follow my lead and try not to look as scared as we both are. We never paid that much for these ponies in the first place, and Na-déné don't go in for rape all that much."

It would have been cruel to tell her, if she didn't know, how the Indians staring at them stone-faced tended to treat *all* white eyes when they were on the warpath. As they rode closer to the long line of Indians, Longarm took a little comfort, but not too much, in the fact that none had painted that white stripe across his face just below his eyes. Their lacking paint was only small comfort because the breed that knew itself as Na-déné, whether described as Apache or Navaho by the Bureau of Indian Affairs, was notorious for taking advantage of any opportunities as they arose. Depending on what seemed to work the best at the time, they were willing to try hunting, farming, trading, raiding, or just murder for practice as far as their neighbors, red, white, or *mestizo,* could see. The word "Apache" was an Indian word, bestowed on those Na-déné bands who'd taken less to raising peaches and sheep than the Na-déné called Navaho, or "gardeners" in the same Pueblo dialect. Apache meant "enemy" in the precise Pima pronunciation that first the Mexicans and then the Anglos had adopted. The Na-déné weren't native to Apacheria, and it showed. They'd wandered south from Totem Pole Country where they'd live a totally different way. Nobody knew why. Their own creation myths involving Spider Woman were just silly. But some language professor had noted it was interesting that a nation that had broken away from the salmon-fishing Déné or plain "People" of the Pacific Northwest liked to call itself *Real* People and refused with vigor to eat fish.

It was known more certainly that the Absaroke or Crows had once been the Sparrow Hawk Clan of the Lakota, but split off to become their bitter enemies after a religious argument about marriage rites.

But whatever the lost history of the so-called Apache, Longarm knew most Indians east of the Continental Divide used the same sign language invented by the Kiowa as a horse-trading jargon on the High Plains.

So as they approached the silently waiting Indians, Longarm raised his right hand to point at them with his trigger finger and middle finger together, before he raised his hand to face level to show them the heel of his palm with those two brotherly fingers pointed up at the sky like two pals standing together.

An Apache on a pale pony was the only one who moved a muscle. He raised his left hand to hold it palm down at chest level to his left side, meaning, "Just you wait right there while we think this over."

So Longarm translated, or started to, before Geneva moaned, "Oh, shit!" in a most unladylike but mighty sincere tone.

Longarm didn't ask why. He could see those other eight or ten Indians coming up behind them from the southeast, while even more sat the rise down that way to account for all that dust against the afternoon sky.

But the scouts out ahead of that party swung wide of Longarm and Geneva to ride on up and report to the boss Indian who'd signed for them to wait and see.

That was all they could do until the Indians had powwowed a mite, and then their chief signed Longarm to advance and be recognized. He did this by beckoning them to come closer as a white kid might, then touching one finger to his earlobe to indicate he was willing to hear. As the two whites rode up the slope, trying not to let their feelings show, the Indian on the pale horse held out both hands, palms down, then moving them up and down as if he was signing, "Thank you."

They found out why once they were within easy earshot and the chief said, in Mission Spanish, "I am called Alejandro. I am still a follower of White Painted Woman because I think your Jesus Chindi was woman-hearted. We are not afraid to fight. But these young men I sent to see what you people had been up to in that canyon tell me you seem to have killed Gordo Vasquez and three more of his *cazadores de humanidad*. Could this be true?"

Since Alejandro had already described Gordo and his bunch as scalp hunters were described by some, Longarm figured it was best to tell the truth when it seemed to be in his favor. So he told the older man the whole story of his brush with Gordo, and added, "I thought Mexico no longer paid that bounty on the scalps of your people, with all due respect to how dangerous they can still be."

Alejandro nodded soberly and said, "Benito Juarez, being of Indian blood himself, ended that old Spanish custom. Diaz has not seen fit to pay for the scalps of Pueblos and his own Mexican women as some have in the past. I spit in the milk of his mother, but Diaz is not a fool. When I called Gordo Vasquez a hunter of humanity, I was talking about some Real People he murdered and scalped when he was younger. We Real People you choose to call Apache have long memories for to go with our pride and family loyalty. Many of us are now in your debt, White Eyes. So tell us what we can do for you and if is possible we shall *do* it!"

So Longarm carried Geneva on to that Confederate enclave she hailed from, after a sit-down warm supper washed down with Apache *tiswin* or home brew and a few hours of sounder sleep than they'd been getting up until then. As Longarm explained and as Geneva had heard, Na-déné could be trusted not to turn on you once they'd invited you in. Their sometimes-harsh code allowed them to murder any strangers they met just to hear them holler. But for all their ferocious reps, the savage Apache hardly ever told fibs, beat their wives or children, or cut the throat of a sleeping guest.

The Apache just woke the two of them early, as requested, and sent them on their way in the wee small hours to ride into Esperanza Nuevo, Escondijo Yanqui, or whatever the hell you wanted to call it, around seven the next morning when everyone was awake to see what in the hell all the dogs were barking about.

So Longarm was treated to a breakast of Dixie-style grits and gravy at the Wallace spread, once it turned out Geneva had been Miss Geneva Wallace before she'd run off like a fool with that greaser.

Longarm pretended he had no idea what anyone was talking about as Wallace after Wallace trooped in to be introduced to him as a wandering peddler the prodigal daughter of the rambling 'dobe house had met up with riding up from the coach road. They'd agreed ahead of time it might be best to leave out the jealous Ramon or just where Longarm had come by those ponies, pistols, and such he had for sale. Geneva allowed the quality duds and modest bankroll she'd come home with were her just rewards for seeing the light and leaving that infernal Luis her kith and kin had never cottoned to. As soon as he was able, Longarm excused himself to ride on into the main settlement with the goods he had for sale. He and Geneva shook hands and she wished him luck. It might have looked funny if they'd kissed good-bye and when you studied on it, they had nothing get all kissy-faced about, blast their common sense.

Riding another paint he'd chosen that morning, and leading the four ponies he had left, Longarm got on over to such a downtown as they had to offer. A trading post, a smithy, and a cantina run by Mexicans shared a single crossroads with that church everyone went to, except for the few Papist Mexicans around the dinky settlement.

Longarm reined in out front of the trading post first. As he'd expected, the old gray cuss inside with a Robert E. Lee beard and a limp allowed he'd pay the going Mexican prices for all that hardware. Longarm was too polite to ask him how much he intended to mark up the guns, spurs, belt buckles, and such. Gents forced to shop in mining towns or Rebel enclaves far from the nearest rail stop were expected to pay *more* than the going prices.

The old-timer said he'd have a tougher time selling the riding stock in a mountain glen where breeding ponies was the major local industry. But Longarm pocketed the profits of his hardware sale with a smile, and didn't put up a real fuss at the smithy across the way when the blacksmith allowed he'd pay ten dollars a head if Longarm wanted to throw in the fancy Mexican saddles.

He held on to the best pony, that cinnamon-colored *canela* gelding, and pocketed the easy forty dollars he'd made on the others. Along the way he'd asked everyone he'd been able whether they'd seen hide or hair of a redheaded Anglo gal riding with two or more Mexicans. Nobody had so far, and the cantina was about all he had left on a weekday. He knew the local preacher would ask all sorts of questions if anybody pestered him in his manse about strange redheads.

Longarm bellied up to the bar in the shady cantina, and got started on the bourbon and branch water unreconstructed Rebels demanded in even a cantina in Old Mexico. He didn't ask where the skinny little Mexican who served him got real Kentucky bourbon. They weren't all that far from where the Southern Pacific Railroad stopped for water from the Rio Bravo at the border town of Langtry, named for an official of the same S.P.R.R., and not that scandalous English actress Miss Lillie Langtry.

The prices they charged for Kentucky bourbon in Old Mexico were as scandalous as the tales they told about Lillie Langtry and the Prince of Wales. But Longarm hadn't paid shit for all the loot he'd just unloaded, so he was a good sport and never cussed the skinny old Mexican. He snapped a Mexican double eagle on the bar and said to quit serving once that much, less a ten percent tip, had been consumed in the form of food and drink. He wasn't ready for any chili yet, thanks to all the grits and gravy he'd been served at the Wallace spread that morning.

He asked the *cantinero,* loud enough to be overheard, about that missing redhead, allowing he'd heard this lady he knew from Texas had last been heard from heading their way with some *vaqueros*.

The old Mexican shook his head and denied serving any such travelers. He seemed sincere as he added that hardly any strangers ever rode through without stopping there for at least a soft drink and some directions. So Longarm took him at his word, and it was sure starting to look as if Perrita had been right about them flimflamming the kidnapped Fiona Palmer into leaving that red-herring message for everyone to find.

He was working on his second drink, wondering what he was supposed to do about that, when a cadaverous individual in a frock coat and planter's hat sidled up to inquire in an oily tone if he might be the North Range rider who'd carried that Wallace gal home from wherever.

Longarm was aware of the Navy Colt conversion with its ivory grips peeking shyly out from under that lavender-gray frock coat as he smiled thinly and replied, "If you'd be talking about the Colorado crush of my Stetson, we wear our hat crowns low where the winds blow wilder for the same reasons Mexicans and Texicans wear their hats high-crowned where you have to worry more about the hot sun beating down on your heads as you ride."

The local intimidator purred, "I could already tell you wore your pestiferous hat in a Colorado crush. I asked you a polite question about that wanton Geneva Wallace, friend."

Longarm stepped away from the bar, and it got mighty quiet in the dinky cantina when Longarm flatly declared, "You ain't no friend of mine, nor, I suspect, of the lady you're so nosy about. Neither a friend nor any sort of gentleman asks questions or answers questions about a lady behind her back."

The scrawny but well-armed cuss in the planter's hat sneered, "Do you call Geneva Wallace a lady? Well, I reckon that explains your own delusions of quality, cowboy."

Longarm counted at least half a dozen sets of local ears listening sharp. So he set his shot glass on the bar to refill it with his left hand as he quietly replied, "*My* quality ain't the subject of this debate. I've been keeping score and I make it three times you've low-rated a lady whose kin have broken bread with me. That's all I know or care for certain about an Esperanza Nuevo lady I only met up with on the trail in from the coach road. I escorted her home through an Indian scare, and that's all I'd be able to say about her if I was a total fool looking for trouble. Why are *you* looking for trouble, Total Fool? Don't you have any better chores to tend to on a working day? What do you do for a living? Might you be a tinhorn gambler or just the sweetheart of a rider who can't get fixed up with a *woman*? Is that why you're so spiteful about another popular beauty, you pretty little thing?"

Somebody laughed. His would-be tormentor gasped, "Nobody talks to me like that and lives! You take that right back or *draw,* you son of a bitch!"

So Longarm threw a shot of bourbon in his face to blind him, and then he backhanded the mean-mouthed priss to the dirt floor, messing his pretty duds considerably, and then kicked his fancy hat off when he whimpered for his gun.

Leaving his own .44-40 holstered, Longarm straddled the downed dude to hunker on top of him and take his ivory-gripped Colt away from him. Then he rose to his own considerable height and announced, "I let this poor simp live because I feel sure his momma would miss him. I hope nobody here has the false impression that a man who doesn't want a fight don't know *how* to fight."

A voice from the rear soberly declared, "It wasn't our fight, mister. We all saw Junior Clayburn picked a fight with *you*. But if I was you I'd ride right now."

Longarm said, "I was fixing to. I've done all I ever come here to do. So I reckon I'll just quit while I'm ahead and mosey on now."

Another local rider volunteered, "You don't want to *mosey,* pilgrim. You want to ride for your life right now, because you can't quit after knocking Junior Clayborn or any Clayborn on his ass. Don't let Junior Clayborn here encourage no false sense of security. Junior talks so brave and hasty because nobody in Esperanza Nuevo wants to tangle with his *brothers,* see?"

Longarm sighed and said, "I'm commencing to. How many brothers does this asshole run with?"

The first helpful voice replied, "Seven. Every last one of them bigger, tougher, and even meaner!"

Chapter 18

Longarm crossed the Rio Bravo a mile upstream of Langtry, Texas, clinging to the cinnamon tail of his mount with his boots and duds lashed to the saddle. He'd chosen that crossing because Langtry was a jerkwater stop for the S.P.R.R. and there was no border town worth mentioning on the Mexican side of the brawling brown Rio Bravo, which became the Rio Grande once you'd crossed it.

Aside from being anxious to throw any other riders off his trail, Longarm knew Perrita and her bloodhounds would have reported back by now, and if El Pico had even one two-face in with Blondita, he'd likely be feeling mighty smug about the gringo lawman he'd sent off on a wild-goose chase. So with any luck, the rascals writing ransom notes about redheads wouldn't be expecting him back for a spell. Longarm knew, and he knew El Pico knew, that even after finding Escondijo Yanqui quickly and giving up on it quickly, a pissed-off lawman ought to spend a long hard spell in the saddle getting back to Ciudad Acuña. So when Longarm rode into the much closer railroad stop of Langtry, he sold his gelding cheap, for more than he'd ever paid for it, and toted his saddle and possibles over to the sun-silvered railroad dispatch shack to ask how soon the next eastbound for Del Rio would be stopping for its engine water. When they told him he had less than forty minutes to wait, he decided against that cold beer advertised just up the way, and moved down to where the afternoon sun cast long shadows across the western end of the platform. He was seated there beside his McClellan, with his legs hanging over the edge, when a familiar figure, riding with a younger cowhand, caught up with him.

Reining in to dismount as Longarm stood up, Geneva Wallace, in a fresh riding habit of summerweight tan shantung, said she'd heard Longarm had raced out of her tiny town and figured he might have headed for Langtry. She handed her reins up to her mounted escort, and accepted the carpetbag he handed down to her before she explained, "That poet who wrote there was no place like home must have had some narrow-minded hellfire-and-damnation place like Esperanza Nuevo in mind. I'd forgotten how *unique* things were back yonder."

She smiled up at the kid she'd ridden in with and said, "*Vete con Dios* and thanks, Miguelito. Remember what I said about telling anyone where I went."

The vaguely Latin-looking kid dressed like an Anglo buckaroo shyly asked, "You *went* somewhere, Miss Geneva? Is funny. I had not noticed."

Then he was riding off with both ponies. So Longarm asked her if she had a train to catch.

As he helped her up on the platform she replied, "With you, if you don't already have somebody else, Custis. I was already thinking about what you'd said about it being sort of pointless to go on running from bluebellies who weren't really after you, and that was before I heard about you knocking Junior Clayborn down for low-rating me, and then getting blamed by my own kin for putting them at feud with the trashy Clayborns in the first place! I want you to show me my own native land, Custis! I haven't seen any of it since I was too young to savor it!"

Longarm bent over to pick up their baggage as he heard a distant railroad whistle. Then he soberly told her, "I don't have any other gal we'd have to answer to. But I've been leaving out who I really have to answer to. I'm a United States deputy marshal on a field mission. When we met I was trying to cut the trail of some Mexican kidnappers, and I only left your tiny home town because they weren't there. It wasn't because I got into trouble fighting for your honor, no offense."

She dimpled up at him and said, "Thank heavens. I'd been worried you might be on the *run* from the law. And you did knock Junior Clayborn to the floor for low-rating me. Friends of me and mine who were there saw you do it, and I'd be proud to help you catch those Mex outlaws, Custis."

He smiled fondly down at her, shook his head, and told her, "They offered to send other deputies along to back my play. I told them what I'm telling you, Miss Geneva. I work better alone. Our eastbound is coming in. I'll be getting off just down the line at Del Rio, and you may as well ride on for New Orleans or at least Galveston, seeing you want to savor the post-war states a mite."

They were still arguing about it as he helped her aboard the Southern Pacifice with her carpetbag. He insisted on paying both their fares at least as far as San Antone, and once they were seated, jawed with her about the jobs for young ladies in these late Victorian times. But as the train slowed down for Del Rio, all too soon when you considered how long it would have taken on horseback, Geneva suddenly grabbed his hand to murmur, "One night! One night of love is all I ask, Custis! I don't want to go back to Mexico. I promise not to follow if you really want to leave me after just one night in Del Rio!"

He sighed and said she was asking a man to eat just one peanut or take just one sip from a jug of cider on a mighty hot day. But she got off at Del Rio when he did. So he decided, "Since we're going to feel dumb if we do and dumb if we don't, I do know this hotel that's open through La Siesta and changes the bedding betwixt guests. But you sure are being forward for a hard-shell Baptist, Miss Geneva!"

She said, "I know. It must be something I et, or all those nights alone waiting for my *prince* until I was just about ready to get down and dirty with a *frog*!"

So they got a room in the Sam Houston, and she got down and dirty with his old organ-grinder, kneeling on the rug between his knees, before they could get all their duds off. When he finally had her naked enough to matter, with a pillow under her flamenco-dancing hips and her shapely dancer's legs opened wide in welcome, it sure felt odd to pound a gal to glory with her spurs jingling in his ears. But as she'd remarked when he'd offered to pull her boots off first, her feet weren't the parts of her that had been gushing for him ever since she'd been staring down at his sleeping face in that faraway canyon in the Serrianas del Burro.

By the time they'd shared a smoke and got going some more, dog-style, she was naturally pestering him to tell her more about Fiona Palmer and where those Mexicans might be holding her.

Moving slowly with a hipbone gripped in either hand as he stared down at the ever-new and inspiring sight of a woman's bare ass, Longarm told her, "All I know for certain now is that they never took her to what she described as Escondijo Yaqui. I doubt they'd want to hold her farther west than the Burros because it would be tough to dicker for that ransom with her clean out of their easy reach. On the other hand, *los rurales,* the Texas Rangers, and my own outfit bought them hiding her *somewhere* out of town because it can be tough to hide an Anglo captive with flaming red hair in a working-class Mexican *barrio*."

Geneva asked if it wasn't possible they were holding her in some dark cellar, then asked him to move in her faster as she speculated on whether the poor redhead was still alive at all.

Longarm got a firmer grip on her hipbones, and began to gyrate in her throbbing innards as he replied in a conversational tone, "They surely know how tough it would be to swap six hundred carbines and a hundred thousand rounds of .45-70 for nothing much. The only way a swap like that could be made, with both governments dead set against the deal, would have to involve some moonlight negotiations close to one side of the border or the other. Either side could be considering a double cross. But simply swapping the gal for the ransom in good faith has a moonlit gunfight with no certain outcome beat by far."

She moaned that she was coming. So he rolled her on her back to finish right, and once she'd done so, with her legs wrapped around him, he insisted on hauling her spurred riding boots off, dad blast 'em, as she giggled and asked if it wouldn't save a lot of money to just gun the Mexicans and take the redhead without giving them such expensive guns and ammunition.

As he tossed her boots aside and flopped down beside her, Longarm said, "Such a ransom in kind wouldn't cost as much as you might think. Those old trapdoor Springfields can be had wholesale for less than ten dollars apiece, and the army only pays ten dollars a thousand, or a penny a round, for factory-fresh .45-70. What say we share another three-for-a-nickel cheroot and . . . Now that's sort of odd, once you study on it."

She snuggled up to him, saying, "Lord have mercy, I'd forgotten how nice it can be in bed with a friendly gent instead of a brute. What's so odd, dear heart?"

He fumbled for the fresh tobacco and matches as he explained. "I just now noticed how little the Palmers would be laying out, in hard cash, if either Mexico City or Washington approved the deal. El Pico has sure stuck his neck out for six thousand dollars worth of single-shot carbines and a thousand dollars worth of ammunition. Old Big Dick could raise three or four times that amount of ransom without going into hock if he had to. I wonder what makes El Pico so willing to work cheap!"

The gal who'd been dancing for her supper all over Mexico told him, "That's easy. Seven thousand dollars looks like a lot more money down Mexico way. You can live like a king down yonder for what a top hand expects as day wages up this way. I know this because I heard as much whilst I was working for centavos and expected to service the management during my Mexican travels."

He didn't ask her how often she'd had to screw anyone down Mexico way. She'd certainly never learned to fornicate like a devil and enjoy it like an angel by playing with herself.

Before she could ask who'd taught him to grind *his* hips the way she said she really liked it, Longarm said, "If you heard about the prices up this way whilst wandering down yonder, a Mexican holed up in a border town ought to have some grasp of international finance, and so what does it mean? Why go to so much trouble and have both federal governments agog over the deal when he could have simply asked for enough *cash* to just buy such guns and ammunition on the market?"

As he lit the cheroot, Geneva suggested a notorious Mexican outlaw might have a time shopping for anything in Texas.

But Longarm snorted, "*Por como?* He's the leader of a *gang*. I doubt he shops for his own tobacco, down Mexico way or anywhere else. So he could enlist any number of more innocent-looking Mexicans, or even someone such as yourself, to go anywhere in the States and just buy all the guns and ammuntion he'd need with hard ransom cash, saving all this State Department anguish. Have you ever been working on a puzzle and suddenly noticed you had some leftover pieces you just couldn't find a place to fit 'em in?"

She sat up in bed, the sunlight through the jalousies sort of tiger-striping her perky-titted torso as she blazed, "Are you intimating I might be in cahoots with Mexican crooks, Custis?"

He said sincerely that the thought had never occurred to him. But once she'd put the thought in his head, he had to admit she might have a point.

As any lawman could tell you, folks with guilty feelings were always sneaking around the edges of a full confession as they asked the lawman they were talking to how much he suspected.

As they cuddled and smoked, Longarm went back over the way they'd met and the things they'd said and done since she'd approached him on the owlhoot trail with those handy directions to that mysterious settlement nobody else could direct him to.

But still, there really had been a place called Escondijo Yanqui, and he didn't see how she could have planned that gunfight with Gordo or meeting up with the friendly Apache Alejandro, and she sure gave a man a mighty sweet time in bed. So he figured he'd keep an open mind, and as if she'd read his mind, she rolled over to open her mouth and swallow him alive to the hilt, with her pointy tongue licking his *huevos.*

Finding it tough to smoke and come at the same time, Longarm put out his cheroot to put his old organ-grinder back in her some more. For some reason this got her to crying, and he asked how come as he kissed the lids of her tear-filled blue eyes.

Thrusting her trim hips in a savage flamenco rhythm as she clung to him like a lost child, Geneva sobbed, "This is so lovely, and you said we could only do it this one time, and, oh, Custis, would you let me *love* you, really love you, for just this one little slice out of forever?"

He thrust back in time with her as he said, "I follow your drift and if you like, I'll really love you back this afternoon. It ain't hard to love a beautiful woman, even when you ain't about to come in her, and looking on the bright side, in times to come, neither one of us will ever look back in anger at the mutual pleasure we're enjoying in the here and now!"

She moaned, "Don't be cruel! Don't remind me that I once loved the lowlife I left home with as much as any woman could ever love any man! It *was* like this in the beginning! I'd forgotten the good times we had. When a man abuses a woman, he spoils all such sweet memories the way pissing in a jar of honey might! So *chinge me. Chinge me mucho* and promise you won't piss in my memories of you, *querido mio*!"

So he tried not to. He made love to her in broad daylight until he felt like he was just showing off, and she was so tired she fell asleep the moment he took it out with a long lingering kiss.

He was tempted to catch a few winks on the pillow beside her own after such a frisky ending to La Siesta. But parting could be such a sweet pain in the ass, and he knew he'd never have a more graceful crack at the best exit line of all.

So he rolled off the bed to dress without disturbing her, picked up his McClellan, Winchester and all, and eased for the door on the balls of his booted feet to make the best exit line of all.

He shut the door softly after him, without saying a fucking word.

Chapter 19

When he got to the Western Union near the Del Rio depot, Longarm was glad he'd saved a day in the saddle and sorry he hadn't gotten there sooner. For the wires they were holding for him there said Hell in a hack was headed for that modest county seat and border crossing.

Big Dick Palmer was on his way in a casket filled with ice and rock salt, on orders of Doc Morrison in conjunction with the Val Verde County Coroner, because after one day on his feet after an apparent recovery, he'd been found dead in his bed after an apparent relapse. They were bringing him down from the Lazy P on ice because embalming fluid could play hob with any other poisons in a body, and Billy Vail wanted Longarm to attend the inquest and wire the results direct to the Vail house up on Denver's Capitol Hill, day or night, no matter what they were.

It got worse. Billy Vail and Washington were more worried about the missing redhead's two brothers, military men missing from their posts and believed to be headed for that border crossing with blood in their eyes and Schofield .45's on their hips.

Neither one of the brothers Maguire had told their superiors their exact plans. But Vail was sure, and Longarm agreed, that those armed and pissed-off Irishmen, looking for the man who'd grabbed their Fiona, were likely to complicate international relations a lot. So Longarm's latest orders were to take off the gloves and bring the abducted bride back dead or alive while the U.S. Government still had some control of the situation.

Longarm didn't know how much control anybody had, but toting his saddle on foot, he crossed back into Ciudad Acuña aboard the crowded ferry raft in the tricky light near sundown, and found it easy to steer clear of the two *rurales* loafing on the landing as he and a mess of homeward-bound Mexicans barged ashore.

As their title indicated, *los rurales* mostly ranged the border, byways, and open country of a mostly rural Mexico. So once you got past the river crossing, you only had to worry about the easier going *policía municipal,* and they didn't seem to give a shit unless you chased wagon wheels and bit folks on their legs.

This time he was relieved of his load and carried right up to La Blondita. Likely because she'd been sitting in a bay window overlooking the *calle* he'd thought he was sneaking along.

Longarm found her fresh from a tub bath with the wet blond hair on her head bound up in a Turkish towel. The rest of her blond hair was drying naturally as she sat on her window seat with one leg up, one leg down, and her robin's-egg-blue silk kimono hanging wide open.

Mexican folklore held that that shade of blue kept flies away. She might have been trying to attract honey bees with all that musky tuberose perfume. But he didn't see any buzzing about as he sat down beside her to say she sure smelled pretty.

La Blondita asked, "How did you like for to fuck Perrita?"

Longarm calmly said he was glad Perrita and her dogs made it back. La Blondita said, "*Los rurales* have those murders under investigation. Is what *los rurales chingado* call riding around in big circles while they curse and shoot off their *pistoles,* investigating. *No es de la primera.* I wish for to know if that *mestiza* is as good a *chingadera* as myself!"

Longarm patted her bare thigh and replied, "I never said I was in any position to say, Miss Blondita. Before those *rurales* killed another unfortunate in my place and I had to change some plans, I'd asked if you could set up a sit-down with El Pico to discuss that redhead and those guns, remember?"

She took his wrist to move his hand further along her thigh as she replied, "*Sin duda.* He accepted our invitation for to meet you in a cantina in the *barrio* neither of our *cuadrillas* control. But of course he called the meeting off when he heard you had been shot crossing El Rio. You wish for us to see if we can set up another meeting with him for you?"

Longarm said, "No. I want him to go on hoping I'm still dead. But just how might anyone from your bunch go about setting up such a set-down in no-man's-land, Miss Blondita?"

She shrugged, exposing even more of her breastworks, and replied, "Is not too *dificil* when one knows where his, how you say, lookouts are posted in his part of Ciudad Acuña. One of my *muchachos* gives one of his *muchachos* a note. They naturally say they have never heard of this El Pico. But then when they are certain nobody is watching, they seem to remember for where to take it. They send us messages the same way."

Longarm started to consider some more complicated ways before he suddenly brightened and decided, "Even better! Might you have any recent love letters from El Pico?"

La Blondita sniffed, "I would rather make love to a reasonably clean pig. But *sí,* I naturally kept the message El Pico sent us about *you.* Do you wish for to read it for yourself?"

Longarm moved his hand the other way as he felt damp pubic hair with his fingertips and replied, "I want both Perrita's bloodhounds to sniff it good. Bruja and Brujo know how you and your bunch smell. If they can still smell anything of El Pico, or even the messenger boy who handed it to *your* messenger boy, and we can sneak through enemy parts of town in the wee small hours, when even you Mexicans are in bed, no offense . . ."

"I knew you were looking for an excuse for to get Perrita alone in the dark with you again!" La Blondita pouted, adding, "You can tell me. I am not, how you say, jealous. I only wish for to know how her *cosita* compares with my own!"

Longarm relaxed and let her haul his hand into her lap as he smiled fondly and confessed, "I think your fuzzy little ring-dang-doo is just swell and you know that, Miss Blondita. But would you want me telling Miss Perrita or anyone else how I'd learned such things about you?"

La Blondita began to pet herself with his hand as she purred, "*Ay, tengo el culo caliente!* But as I told you the last time, my position forces me to be most discreet and I am so happy you are not a . . . how do you say, *besar y desir*?"

Longarm told her, "*We* say kiss and tell. It ain't considered all that manly where I come from."

La Blondita suddenly shoved his hand out of her crotch and rose to move over by a black velvet chaise longue and pull a bell cord on the wall behind it as she coyly confessed, "Perrita told me you never said a word about my . . . personal habits to her while you were in that bedroll with her. Not even after you have come in her and were sharing a smoke and most friendly conversation. That is the time most lovers are going to confess their sins, or boast about them. Yet even though you could have said you had taken all the famous La Blondita had for to offer, you never did. You are like those three wise monkeys when it comes to *amor y compañia* and I like that in an *hombre*. Is *inspirar* for to feel that no matter how *perverso* one wishes for to act, one's *own* little secrets will be safe, *comprende*?"

Longarm rose from the window seat to unbuckle his gun rig as he replied, "I reckon. It's early yet, and I don't want to take those two bloodhounds into enemy territory until at least four in the morning."

He was expecting something French or Greek, and wondering if he'd be up to the job so soon after that session with a blue-eyed brunette.

Then another gal came in in response to La Blondita's summons, as naked as a jay and fresh from her own tub bath, but smelling more of that sandalwood perfume you smelled in Chinese curio shops.

That was fair. She looked to be pure Chinese until she giggled and confided in Spanish, *"Ay, Dios mio, imagino que es un amante tremendo y sabe chichar como toro!"*

So La Blondita confirmed that the male member of the three-way orgy they'd gotten all cleaned up for was indeed a great lover who knew how to rut like a bull, and introduced the naked Oriental as private stock called La Sinverguenza, which in Border Mexican could signify a tramp or just a gal you couldn't shame.

He saw what La Blondita meant about private stock when she got rid of her kimono entirely and the two gals got down on the black chaise longue together, in what Mexicans described as the *sesenta y nueve* or *al reverso* position. Where Longarm came from it was just called sixty-nine, and while nobody was allowed to do it in some states, it was considered more natural for a man and a woman, not two men or two women, to pleasure one another that way.

As the more willowy Chinese gal got on top with her Oriental face in La Blondita's lap and her tawny rump staring the bigger blonde in the face, La Blondita asked him, "For why do you hesitate? Does this shock you too much for to get it up for La Sinverguenza?"

Longarm sat back down to shuck his boots as he confided, "I doubt anything could shock me enough to refuse such a tempting offer. But how could you have ladies known I was on my way here this evening?"

La Blondita confided, "We didn't. We were about to start without you when you honored us with this unexpected visit. As I have said, I have to be most discreet with my male followers. But a woman with an adventurous mind and a *cosita caliente* takes advantages of those opportunities that come her way. So come first in this Chinese *culo* while she eats me, and then you can *chinge* me while I lick away the sins of both of you."

By the time Longarm had finished undressing and risen, both ways, both gals were slurping too wildly to carry on any conversations. So Longarm strode over to the chaise longue, braced bare feet wide on the Oriental carpet, and grabbed the Oriental gal by the hips to thrust into her with the help of La Blondita's helping hand.

La Sinverguenza gasped in mingled surprise and pleasure as she went on licking La Blondita's clit. The bigger white gal laughed and allowed that that felt *muy perverso,* and confessed it also felt wicked to stare up at another gal taking it dog-style at such close range while she was having her own *chocha* kissed in the manner of las lesbianas.

All Longarm knew was that it sure felt swell in the end of the Chinese gal who *wasn't* acting lesbian.

It felt swell when it was La Blondita's turn to get on top too. After having shoved it in three totally different gals since last they'd met, he found the throbbing innards of the hot and bothered blond Mexican almost new, and before it was over he'd gotten to lay them in turn the good old-fashioned way—with La Sinverguenza a tad nicer, belly-to-belly, if the truth be told, in spite of or mayhaps because she seemed a tad confused to be in such an unfamiliar position with a natural man.

But he never told either gal he liked anyone best, and a good time was had by all, even though La Sinverguenza took to crying and saying he had her confused after he'd made her come the old-fashioned way, while La Blondita kept nagging him not to tell anyone what they'd been up to, even when he pointed out they were still up to it and there was nobody else around to tell.

Then the three of them ate a late supper in the Hispanic manner. Not having to entertain Texicans or tourists, La Blondita served up some real Mexican food, such as chicken glazed with chocolate, fried bananas, and such, with the *hilado vainilla* served after ten P.M. and the Chinese gal blowing him while he kissed La Blondita for an extra dessert.

Then they all caught some sleep in La Blondita's four-poster in the other room, and when she woke Longarm up after three to say Perrita was downstairs with her bloodhounds, but that they had just enough time for a quick one, he told her to hold the thought, and went out to gather up his duds and put them on, along with his more important six-gun. For a man could wander the streets of Ciudad Acuña in the wee small hours wearing a six-gun but no pants a whole lot safer than he could get away with wearing a three-piece suit with no side arm.

La Blondita joined him out there, bare-ass, to give him that note from El Pico and a kiss for luck.

Downstairs, by the casually but always guarded patio gate, he found little Perrita and her bloodhounds waiting. He kissed her and ducked into the gatekeeper's cubby to take his Winchester and that chemise Fiona Palmer had worn from his saddle. He told the Mexican on guard duty he'd be back in due time for the rest, Lord willing and the creeks didn't rise or La Revolucion didn't start before he could return.

Somewhere in the dark a clock was chiming four A.M., but this being Mexico, there were still folks up and about, although not nearly as many as there'd been at three or figured to be by five. Perrita knew her own town better than she'd known the open country to the west. So he let her steer him and the leashed bloodhounds into some mighty dark and creepy streets indeed, downwind of the big bull ring that was only open for those moments of truth on the weekends. They'd told Perrita which dark corner to scout. There didn't seem to be anybody from any gang at the dark intersection at that hour. Longarm handed their handler the wadded message from El Pico. Perrita let her *sabuesos* snuffle and slurp the already messy paper before she murmured, "*Vamanos, perros!*" and the two of them commenced to circle, snuffle, and slurp: at the pavement until Bruja suddenly gave a soft whuff and led the rest of them into an alley entrance as Perrita chortled, "She has picked up a scent! Is down this way, *muy fuerte*! At least one of the *cabrones* who handled that paper must travel back and forth along this *paseo*."

Longarm didn't ask whether she could tell if they were tracking El Pico himself or just a follower. He knew she couldn't. It didn't matter. For just as all roads led to Rome, all followers led to the son of a bitch they followed if you followed them far enough.

In this case the bloodhounds followed the scent-trail for almost a quarter mile, with the hornier but not as keen Brujo joining in as the scent seemed to be getting stronger.

Human beings might have gone right past the section of high board fence between what seemed two warehouses with their back doors to yet another dimly lit alley. But when both hounds stopped to pant and stare at what seemed a solid eight-foot fence, Longarm pushed on one plank, then another, until he suddenly smiled grimly and opened the simple but invisible gate the hounds had led him to.

Perrita whispered, "Be careful, *querido*! We are deep in El Pico's *barrio* and he could be lurking just inside!"

To which Longarm could only reply, "I sure hope so. It's about time I caught up with that son of a bitch!"

Chapter 20

The bloodhounds led them along a dirt footpath across a weed-grown empty lot to the rear of a two-story 'dobe building facing the *calle* on the far side of the block. A sliver of light from a street lamp shone through an arched-over passageway offering a more natural way around to the front. The bloodhounds began to mill at the foot of a wooden stairway leading up to the second story. Perrita whispered, or started to. Longarm whispered, "I can see there's a regular way and a sneaky way in or out. Stay put and let me scout that more public service entrance."

She moved into the niche of a first-floor doorway under the dark shadows of the stairway, with Bruja and Brujo, as Longarm followed the muzzle of his Winchester around a corner and just a ways along that passageway out to the front. Then he froze when he heard voices.

One male voice complaned, *"Que hora es? Tengo hambre!"*

When another man assured him they would be relieved for to go have some breakfast within the hour, Longarm crawfished around to the back to rejoin Perrita, murmuring, "Talk about your weak links in even the strongest chain! They got the front guarded. But they must think that sneakier way in is an iron-bound secret wonder!"

He took the missing redhead's underwear from his pocket and asked their handler what the bloodhounds might have to say about that.

Perrita let them both sniffle and slobber to their heart's content, but neither Bruja nor Brujo seemed inspired to sniff anywhere else for her in that dark backyard. So the petite Indian gal assured him, "She has never been back here. Had they taken her in through that back door or up those stairs, my *sabuesos* would tell us. Is easy for to track where not too many others are in the habit of walking."

He asked how she felt about them taking the kidnapped gal inside by way of that guarded front entrance. Perrita led both bloodhounds to the back door and whispered to them. They both sniffed along the doorstep, but then they stared up at her reproachfully, as if asking her why she was wasting their time when they could be digging up bones.

She told Longarm, "If she had spent any time inside, some of her scent would settle to the bottom floor and seep under the door within a day or so, and she has been missing many days, no?"

Longarm struck a match. The bottom door was padlocked, as if it led to some ground-floor business or storage space. He shook out the light and decided, "I'd best have a creep up those stairs."

Perrita protested, "*Cono no*! Is the *escondijo de El Pico*! Would you walk right into a wolf's den alone with your eyes wide open?"

To which he modestly replied, "Better to do it with your eyes open than with 'em both shut. You-all run along now, if you're scared, Miss Perrita. I reckon me and my guns can take over from here."

She hesitated, then said, "*Lo siento, querido*. You are simply too much of a *toro chingado* for me and my *sabuesos* to play with!"

Longarm said, "*Esta bien,*" and started up the stairs on the balls of his feet. When he got to the landing and looked around, Perrita and her bloodhounds were nowhere down yonder to be seen. That sure made a man feel lonely, standing there with the sky starting to pearl in the east and nary a sound coming from the dark side of that nail-studded oaken door.

Cradling the Winchester over one elbow, Longarm gingerly tried the latch, and finding it locked, got out his pocket knife and got to work with a blade he'd had reworked by a Denver locksmith who hadn't wanted to do it.

The stout but simple latch surrendered after a few moments. Longarm put the knife away and had the Winchester trained more hostilely as he eased the door open and followed the muzzle into a dark dining room. He knew any kitchen they had would be down on the first floor. Somewhere in the upstairs quarters a clock chimed the half hour after four and a sleepy male voice called out, *"Que pasa?"*

Longarm moved closer, but waited until he heard soft snoring before he moved in on the front bedroom the human sounds had come from. That door was locked as well. Sleeping on a guilty conscience could inspire lots of locks as well as round-the-clock guards downstairs.

The snoring helped Longarm as he picked that lock in turn. Aside from covering any slight clicks he might make, the steady snoring had a soothing effect on his nerves as he worked at a real pisser, knowing he wasn't in real trouble as long as the cuss inside kept snoring.

But when he finally managed to ease the bedroom door open, there was this Mexican gal sitting upright with her naked spine to the head of the bed, staring wide-eyed at the tall, tanned lawman holding the muzzle of his saddle gun on her. She didn't move to cover her bare tits in the lamplight from out front as she stared up at him like a sparrow-bird transfixed by a tree snake.

Beside her snored what sort of resembled a beached whale, until you noticed it was a big fat slob who sure seemed self-indulgent. Longarm could see why they called him El Pico. Even flat on his back he looked like a mountain of lard, dressed in nothing at the moment but his oily unwashed hide.

The woman quietly murmured, "Please do not kill me, Señor. I could have awakened him as you were picking the lock for so long. But as you see, I did not."

Since she'd addressed him in fair English, Longarm asked her in the same lingo why she'd been so good to him.

She shrugged her bare shoulders and replied in a defeated voice, "Was not my desire for to be here, with or without that gun pointed at me. You *all* have guns, and a woman of the people who has nobody must go where she is told and sleep with those they tell her for to sleep with. I know there is a price on this one's head. But I am not worth anything to anybody but myself, dead or alive. So do you really have to kill us both?"

Before Longarm could answer, El Pico ran a palm over his face and groaned, "*Que pasa?* For why are you chattering like a *papagayo,* and who are you talking to, *mi tirada*?"

Then he woke up enough to see what a pickle they were in, and sat up slack-jawed to gasp, *"Ay, Dios mio!"*

To which Longarm modestly replied, "Aw, I ain't your God. I'd only be U.S. Deputy Marshal Custis Long of the Denver District Court."

"*Cono no!* We killed you! I mean *los rurales* killed you, El Brazo Largo!"

Longarm soberly replied, "That's another thing I aim to take up with you, *mi amigo poquito*. But first we're going to talk about your more important victim, Fiona Palmer. Both your government and my own would like me to carry her home. So that's what I'm here for and where is the poor gal, you *estaca de mierda fregada*?"

Then he told the naked gal next to El Pico, "Sorry, ma'am, but he's been mighty mean to this other woman and she does have somebody. He is called Tio Sam and I ride for him."

Neither Mexican answered. So seeing he had their undivided attention, Longarm told El Pico, "If you hope to stall for time until somebody in your gang comes up here with your morning coffee, I ain't giving you that much time. I know I have to get out of here soon. So whether I leave with you and Fiona Palmer still breathing or not is up to you. I give you my word you are fixing to die by the time I count to ten unless you tell me where you're holding that redhead!"

El Pico replied, "As *Jesus, Maria y Jose* are my witnesses, we do not have the *gringa* you seek. We never had her. I would not know this Señora Palmer if I woke up in this bed with her!"

"Two," said Longarm conversationally.

So El Pico insisted, "*Ay, que chihuahua!* Can't you gringos take a joke? We did nothing to that *cabeza roja*! We never laid eyes on the Tejana! *Yo no sé que le pasa al pendejo chocha,* and that is all I can tell you about her!"

"Three," said Longarm, adding, "You got to do better than that. I read the ransom demands you sent to her menfolk."

El Pico protested, *"Enumere despacio, por favor!"* The massive tub of lard pleaded, "You must give me time for to explain! Was not my idea for to hold anyone for ransom. We had nobody for to hold for *mierditas*! We knew nothing of any abduction until that Tejana's people sent us a message saying I was asking for too much!"

"Four!" sighed Longarm, wearily but sincerely.

El Pico slobbered, "*Es verdad! No fue culpa mia!* Let me explain! We were not the ones who kidnapped that Tejana! We don't know who did it! We don't know for why her people thought we were holding her for guns and ammunition. But if some *pendejo* offered you those six hundred carbines and a hundred thousand bullets for to shoot out of them, you would take them, no?"

Longarm said, "No. How could anyone hope to collect any ransom when they had nobody to swap for the same?

I make it five and still counting, you lying *hijo de puta*!"

The woman in bed with the brute swung her bare feet to the floor as El Pico protested, "For why would I lie with a gun in my face if I had the *chingado* woman for to *give* you?"

Longarm said, "Six! I'd like you to stay put, ma'am."

But she slid her bare ass off the bed to move over to her dress, draped over a chair, as she calmly replied, "I did not wish for to be spattered with warm blood and fat when you shot him. I know you are going to shoot him because I have heard them talking about this *mujer misteriosa* and he is not able to answer your questions, and this makes me *muy contenta*. He has bad breath as well."

So Longarm said, "*Bueno,* but don't go no place. Why would anybody else want to kidnap a bride on her honeymoon and send ransom demands to her family?"

El Pico sobbed, "You are holding the answer in your hand, gringo! Was done by my enemies for to get me in trouble! I admit I walked into their trap like a *paloma estupida* following a line of seeds under a box poised on a stick when someone sent word they were willing for to let me have six hundred guns but no more. But that is all I know about this missing *cabeza roja,* and can you not see what they are trying to do here?"

Longarm said, "Seven. You mean something like you were trying for when you got word to *los rurales* I'd be leaving town on a castaña?"

The huge naked slob smiled sheepishly and confessed, "I was afraid when I heard El Brazo Largo wished to talk to me about that *mujer* I could not produce. But they *missed* you. So no harm was done, eh?"

Longarm wasn't smiling back as he said, "Not to me. The kith and kin of a man called Jacobs may want to talk to you about that. So I reckon you'd best start getting dressed your ownself."

El Pico looked puzzled and asked, "We are going someplace, El Brazo Largo?"

Longarm nodded grimly and said, "Texas. We won't be able to ride the ferry because you're too big and famous, literally. But they told me to tidy up this international mess, and a bird in the hand will have to do for now."

"But I am not wanted in Texas!" El Pico protested.

Longarm said, "Yes, you are. For the murder of Laguna Jacobs, no matter who's holding Fiona Palmer. If it's your bunch, we'll have you to barter instead of all those more dangerous Springfields. On the outside chance that you're telling me the truth, we won't be any worse off with you in custody in Texas than running loose down here, so . . ."

Then that two-faced woman Longarm had let off the bed lobbed a Colt .45 from nowhere to her big fat lover as she shouted, *"Coge, querido!"*

So El Pico's first mistake was that he caught the six-gun as she'd directed. His second mistake was that he didn't drop it like a red-hot poker. For before he could point it at the man looming over the foot of the bed with a Winchester, Longarm fired the weapon in his face.

He fired again when the .45 in the giant's hand went off in another direction and that two-faced woman screamed fit to bust.

Longarm fired into the mountain of flesh on the bed some more, and commenced to make tracks without checking to see whether the woman had been hit or not. From all the noise coming out of her smoke-filled corner, she surely had to be still alive!

As Longarm tore out the back door to that second-story landing, two shadowy forms were coming up the stairs at him, yelling questions.

Longarm chased the blazing muzzle of his Winchester down the same stairs to jump over their sprawled bodies and run for that back gate at least a day's ride away. Then, by some miracle, he was on the other side of the city block and walking, not running, with his hot Winchester down at his side like an umbrella while window lamps winked on all around and more questions were shouted back and forth in the dawn's early light.

So it seemed he'd gotten safe away, praise the Lord, but what in blue blazes had that all been about, and if El Pico and his bunch were not holding Fiona Palmer, who in blue blazes was he really after?

It was time to do some of Billy Vail's *eliminating* as Mexicans, who some tourists put down as lazy, got to popping out of doorways like cuckoo-clock birds before sunrise to make up for those lost siesta hours in the heat of the day before. So it got easier to just poke along as if he had some innocent morning errand while his mind ran in far faster circles. That two-faced woman who'd said El Pico was telling the truth had been lying about her feelings toward El Pico. But after that, their story commenced to make more sense than some chess game the Borgias of Old Italy might have found needlessly complicated. Dragging a kidnap victim over twenty miles out of town across open range, where red hair stood out as mighty strange, made little sense if you meant to drag her right back to the same town, and those bloodhounds hadn't been able to pick up a whiff of Fiona Palmer anywhere near El Pico's hideout in his own *barrio*.

In the meantime, he had to pick up his saddle and possibles at La Blondita's and get on across to Del Rio in time to attend that inquest on the sudden death of Big Dick Palmer, so . . .

Sure he did, in a mighty sneaky pig's ass!

It hurt like fire to consider a gal who screwed like La Blondita as another two-faced woman. But once you eliminated one of the two main gangs in Ciudad Acuña, who was left? And he could always send for his old McClellan, spare socks, and such if his sudden suspicions about a self-confessed gang leader with the morals of, well, a whore turned out to be wrong.

Meanwhile, it was just as easy to walk on by and join the morning crowd of day workers heading across the river to Del Rio as the sun came up.

Chapter 21

A politely nosy revenue man stopped Longarm on the ferry landing for Del Rio to remark, "I can see you ain't a greaser, but would you like to tell me why you'd be packing that Winchester with that Colt on your hip, mister?"

There was no need to lie when the truth was in his favor. So Longarm replied, "I couldn't get no Mexicans to carry it for me. I'd be U.S. Deputy Marshal Custis Long, returning from a diplomatic mission to Old Mexico, and I'd be much obliged if you could tell me where they might hold coroner's inquests in Del Rio."

The revenuer said, "County courthouse, I reckon. Would you care to show me some identification, Deputy Long?"

Longarm didn't really care to, but it saved a lot of bother to just flash his damned badge at the nosy cuss and be on his way.

But when he hailed a passing hansom to ride up to the courthouse, the main parts of Del Rio being back from the river's floodplain a bit, the Mexican driver told him it was too early if he meant to talk to anybody there. Longarm recalled Vail wiring that they'd be holding the inquest Friday, and told the driver to drop him off at that hotel by the depot instead.

Once he got there, they let him hire a room with no baggage because he'd stayed there recently with Geneva Wallace. So he got upstairs and caught up on the beauty rest he'd missed while trying to track down missing redheads where no missing redheads were to be found.

He woke up hungry before La Siesta had wound down. So the hotel dining room was closed downstairs. He was hungry as a bitch wolf by the time the sunny streets of the border town cum county seat came back to life. But knowing he'd only wind up famished by supper time if he ate that early, and seeing his shaving kit and such were still in his saddlebags down Mexico way, Longarm stopped by a haberdasher's shop for a fresh shirt, treated himself to a hot tub at a public bath, and went to a barbershop near the depot for a sit-down shave and some bay rum, all to kill time before he ordered supper after five like an honest workingman was supposed to.

Great minds seemed to run in the same channels. He found fat Doc Morrison and another older gent having an early supper there. Morrison invited Longarm to join them, and after confessing he was staying at that same hotel, he introduced the other gray-haired cuss as one of the county coroner's forensic experts. As they shook across the table, the other doctor, called Templer, said they'd just put the late Big Dick Palmer on ice over to County General, and meant to open him up in the cool shades of Thursday Eve before the hearing.

Templer added, "No signs of injury when we undressed him, and we've already tested his soiled duds and bed linens for arsenic. So it's unlikely he was murdered under his own roof, as Doctor Morrison here first feared."

Longarm waited until the weary-looking but sort of pretty Mexican waitress had taken his order for steak and potatoes, as a novelty in those parts, before he asked Doc Morrison why he suspected foul play.

The older man smiled uncertainly and confessed, "Maybe it's only professional pride. He'd been poisoned at that wedding in Comstock with enough arsenic to kill a horse. But he was strong as a bull and the only complications I was worried about, once he was sitting up in bed and eating again, were the usual pneumonia or heart failure such a weakened patient may be prone to."

Doc Templer suggested, "We've asssayed his soiled bed linens for arsenic and other common toxins. The most poisonous chemistry in his crap was chili pepper and alcohol, neither in fatal quantity. When we open him up we'll be able to tell if his lungs are congested or his heart was in bad shape."

Longarm's order arrived, and since the two sawbones were working on their coffees and desserts by then, he let them argue about such really appetizing details while he dug in.

He was putting away the last of the potatoes when Aurora Palmer, the mighty recent widow of the late Big Dick, came in wearing brand-new widow's weeds of black silk and unescorted.

Longarm hadn't known she was staying at the same hotel as well. As the three men rose, the gray-haired but still comely Aurora explained that her stepson, Little Dick, had gone over to the Del Rio federal house of detention to arrange bail for his in-laws, the brothers Maguire.

She sighed and added, "Never try to cross the Mexican border when the U.S. Army has you down as possible deserters. Could you do anything for them, Custis? Seeing you're a federal official?"

Longarm replied, "I'll have a talk with them this evening, ma'am. But it's only fair to warn you I'm a civilian riding for Uncle Sam, not a military police officer."

Doc Morrison signaled that same waitress to fetch them at least two more chairs, and swung his own closer to Templer's so the widow could sit between them as they waited for Little Dick to join them. Longarm sat across from her, next to the empty place they were saving for her stepson, and the waitress had just brought two more chairs and set the extra places at the now-sort-of cozy round table when Little Dick came striding in alone to declare, "It seems you can't bail a suspected deserter out of an army guardhouse. I just now came from a lawyer I know here in town. He says he'll see what he can do."

Then Little Dick became aware of Longarm, and sat down beside him with a hopeful expression to demand, "What's the latest about my poor wife? Where have you been all this time?"

Longarm said, "Eliminating. I got a Mexican pal with bloodhounds and let them sniff Miss Fiona's underwear. The bloodhounds, not the Mex pal."

Aurora blinked in confusion and asked, "How could you have managed to come by any of poor Fiona's unmentionables if you didn't know where she was?"

Longarm explained, "I got 'em where I knew she'd been. Up at your Lazy P, before Little Dick and me rode down this way. I had that maid, Nita, fetch a chemise the missing gal had worn from her clothes hamper."

Little Dick and his stepmother exchanged glances. The dead cattle baron's son asked her thoughtfully, "Didn't you say it was that Mex gal Nita who discovered Daddy dead at dawn? Or the one who said she had?"

Aurora blanched, but said, "Oh, no, not Juanita! I was the one who told her to take him his morning coffee and *tostadas*. We hadn't been sleeping in the same room least I disturb him. But he was feeling better when I served his hot chocolate the night before and . . . No, I can't believe that innocent-looking little thing would or could do anything wicked to a man the size and strength of your poor father, Richard!"

Little Dick shook his head like a bull with a fly between its horns and said, "These medical men are fixing to tell us how my daddy died, Miss Aurora. We were talking about my missing wife!"

Turning back to Longarm, he asked, "What happened after you let them hounds sniff Fiona's underwear?"

Longarm said, "They seemed to find traces of the same scent around those market stalls where you say you last saw her. Then we lost the trail in town, and rode on out to that *posada* where that message from her was found. The bloodhounds had a divided opinion about the corner she was seen seated in by some now-dead witnesses. The handler opined that a public dining room such as this one gathers too many odors over the course of time for the scent of a reasonably clean woman to stand out. But witnesses and at least one bloodhound agreed she'd likely been in that corner long enough to leave that message. So we went on to what she'd misspelled as a *Yaqui* hideout when the local Mexicans called it a *Yanqui* hideout, whilst the unreconstructed Rebels we found there all thought of it as an outpost of the Confederacy."

"So was she there? Or had she been there?" asked the missing woman's visibly excited husband.

Longarm shook his head and said, "Nope. The few Mexicans in and about Esperanza Nuevo, as they called it, were well known to the mostly Anglo and not too numerous local settlers. I pushed on to the nearest border crossing, near Langtry. My Mexican dog handler had turned back by then, but I asked around a dinky jerkwater stop you can see all the way across when the sun is shining, and nobody there recalled a redhead or any other Anglo gal in the company of two or more Mexican riders."

"Then where could they have taken her?" asked the missing gal's stepmother-in-law.

Longarm said, "Not where I next went eliminating, ma'am. Figuring her kidnappers had slickered a victim into leaving us a red herring and then backtracked to the same town they'd kidnapped her from, I used those same bloodhounds to lead me to El Pico's hideout in his own *barrio* of Ciudad Acuña. El Pico assured me with the muzzle of a saddle gun staring him in the eye that they weren't holding Miss Fiona anywhere near, and those bloodhounds on my side backed him up."

Longarm downed the last of his coffee and set the drained mug aside, adding, "If it's any comfort to you, I got El Pico to confess it was him who got Laguna Jacobs shot in my place. So he was doubtless in a sincerely conversational mood as we had our little chat in his hidey-hole."

Little Dick sounded a tad petulant as he snapped, "I'm sure Laguna's Indian squaws will want to settle that score with El Pico. What about *my* wife, damn it?"

Longarm soothingly replied, "I told you El Pico didn't have her, and there's no need for the Jacobses to invade Mexico with the Maguires. I had to eliminate El Pico entirely whilst I was eliminating him as your wife's kidnapper. El Pico told me he suspected the real kidnappers had sent a ransom note from him to your late father just to get him in the mess it did. He said the first he knew of any ransom was when your father tried to beat him down on the price, and seeing it seemed to be found money, El Pico went along with the game. I suspect he regretted his own dishonest dealings towards the end."

Aurora Palmer gasped, "I see it all now, Richard. I warned you two not to honeymoon in that horrid little border town with all the trouble they've been having down Mexico way! You poor children got caught up in some struggle between rival Mexican factions, and I fear I owe her an apology. For Lord knows what's become of poor Fiona, but they never intended to return her for *any* ransom! Don't you agree with me, Custis?"

Longarm replied, "I'm still eliminating, Miss Aurora. I agree those ransom demands were mighty odd to begin with. I never would have wound up with this case if both the U.S. and Mexican governments hadn't gotten wind of an arms shipment to known rebels. Had anyone holding Miss Fiona wanted guns, they could have asked for *cash* and bought their *own* guns without getting everybody so het up."

He shook his head wearily and marveled, "They could have demanded ten thousand in cash and still come out ahead! At ten dollars apiece, those six hundred Springfields could be bought on the open market for six thousand dollars. Those hundred thousand rounds of .45-70's could be bought in bulk for a thousand more. Wouldn't your father have paid a mite more than seven thousand in cash for Miss Fiona, Little Dick?"

The missing redhead's husband snapped, "We'd have paid ten times that much! We told you right off that raising the *money* wasn't the sticking point. It was getting either Washington or Mexico City to go along with paying off in guns and ammunition we were stuck with!"

Aurora insisted, "It was all some sort of sinister game! They never meant to return poor Fiona. They knew my poor late husband would never be allowed to pay such a ransom and they didn't *care*! Oh, can't anyone see what really happened? Isn't it obvious some rival faction kidnapped our poor Fiona and sent ransom demands in El Pico's name just to get him in trouble?"

Longarm said, "It got El Pico killed, and Lord knows how I'll get my saddle back without some awkward explaining now. For that's how I read it myself at first. But after several hours sleep and some time to just sit and think in hot tubs and barber's chairs, it came to me that Mexican rivals out to get El Pico in trouble never would have had to *go* to so much trouble. They'd have simply told *los rurales* where to set up an ambush for El Pico, the way El Pico tried to set *me* up. So after we're finished here in Del Rio, and I doubt that coroner's inquest is likely to uncover much, I mean to ride back to your Lazy P spread with you and some bloodhounds from the county sheriff's department."

"Whatever for?" asked the Widow Palmer. "There's no mystery as to where Fiona went once she left on her honeymoon with Richard here! We saw them off as they rode down this way to some fate unknown for poor Fiona!"

Little Dick swiveled in his chair to face Longarm as he demanded, "Are you saying me and my wife rid somewheres *else* on our honeymoon? Didn't they remember us staying at that *posada*? Didn't that one gal remember Fiona's red hair and green dress in that Mex market where I first noticed she was missing?"

Longarm quietly replied, "Other Mexicans out at that *posada* said they recalled a redheaded *gringa* seated at that corner table too. But one good-looking Anglo gal with red hair, or a red wig, looks a lot like any other Anglo gal with red hair, or a red wig, even to an Anglo witness who's only seen her fleetingly in tricky light. So we'd best just eliminate *that* possible red herring by making sure the lady in question ever *left* the Lazy P to begin with. I noticed when I was out there, no offense, your flooring was tiles laid over tamped-down sand. So what if we just let those bloodhounds sniff Miss Fiona's chemise and see if they can show us where she *really* wound up."

Then silverware was clattering to the floor as Doc Morrison yelled, "No! Miss Aurora! Don't!"

So despite himself Longarm glanced that way just long enough to see both sawbones had the Widow Palmer and her bitty whore pistol under control. But as his eyes swung back to Little Dick, he saw the big spoiled brat was already going for his far more serious six-gun!

Chapter 22

Longarm wore his .44-40 cross-draw even though there was no doubt a cross draw was slower standing face-to-face against a shootist who favored a side draw.

In any *other* position you could cross-draw quicker, and that was just as well this evening because Little Dick Palmer had been working up to a side draw before the distraction, and almost beat Longarm from his seated position as it was.

But almost wasn't good enough when six hundred grains of double-action lead propelled by 120 grains of powder blew you backwards, chair and all, to wind up staring at the pressed-tin ceiling with a bemused smile on your lips, a blank look in your eyes, and three bullet holes in the smoking front of your shirt.

As everyone rose, Aurora Palmer fought free of the doctor holding her .32 Harrington Richardson to circle the table and fall to her knees in the drifting gunsmoke, sobbing, "No, darling! Please don't die after all the plans we've made!"

But as she cradled Little Dick's head in her arms, rocking back and forth in numb confusion, Longarm told her, not unkindly, as he began to reload, "He's already dead, ma'am. I want you to listen to me tight before you tell us any more lies. They may not want to, but they do hang women in the state of Texas, and we've got you cold on a double-barreled charge of premeditated murder whether you help us tie up some loose ends or not."

She sobbed, "I don't know what you're talking about! You're the one who just murdered my Dicky Bird, you fucking killer!"

Longarm insisted, "I know you won't be getting out until you're old enough to really match that prematurely gray hair, Miss Aurora. But confession is good for the soul, and may be good enough for the state of Texas, if I can put in a good word for you. I hope you can see neither one of you secret lovers committed any *federal* crimes. So I have to turn you over to the Rangers, now that nobody has to fret about international incidents."

Doctor Templer, being county law as well as medical, horned in to ask him, "What's this about secret loving? Are you saying that man you just shot was carrying on with his stepmother here?"

Doc Morrison demanded, "Where did you get all these sudden notions about incest and murder, Deputy Long? I swear, I've served as family doctor on call to the Lazy P for years, and I never saw anything that made me suspect anything the least bit unusual until somebody poisoned Big Dick Palmer at that wedding over in Comstock."

Longarm holstered his warm .44-40 without taking his eyes from the weeping widow woman as he quietly asked her, "Would you like to tell him when and where you poisoned your husband, or shall I hazard a guess, Miss Aurora?"

She sobbed, "Go to Hell and *tell* him! I hate you, hate you, hate you all!"

Longarm told the two astounded medical men, "She's distraught. I'd say she slipped some sweetish arsenic trioxide to him in the wedding cake she cut for him over in Comstock. You said yourself it should have killed a horse. They knew that had you docs detected poison as the cause of death, nobody could say who might have slipped it to him at a big gathering far from home. They were too slick to poison him under his own roof. They let him be as long as he was too sickly and weak to catch them playing slap and tickle down the hall. But since they had to finish him off once he commenced to feel better, I'll bet you find his hyoid bone busted when you autopsy him. Hardly anybody knows about that bitty sliver of windpipe bone that gets busted when you choke a man to death."

The doctor who rode for the county coroner said, "Palmer's hyoid may be intact if they *burked* him."

Longarm saw that Doc Morrison seemed confused. So he explained, "Burke and Hare supplied cadavers for this medical school in Edinburgh. That's in Scotland. They got hung after some Scotch lawmen found out they weren't bothering to dig up dead folks. They were *manufacturing* dead folks with a method called burking ever since. Whilst Hare held them helpless, Burke pinched their nostrils shut and covered their mouths with his big sweaty palm until they just gave up trying in vain to breathe and came along quietly to that medical school."

He gently asked the sobbing woman at his feet, "Is that how the two of you finished off your husband, ma'am? You likely noticed how a man being suffocated by any means craps the bed linens more than usual as he's dying. Must have been a nasty jolt for poor little Nita when you sent her in there with that coffee tray."

Their waitress, or someone else who worked there, had run out for some law in the wake of all that gunplay. So as two gents in the blues of the Del Rio police came in, guns drawn, Longarm called out, "It's all over and I'm the federal law. This dead man and this weeping woman in black are under arrest for murder in the first. Or at least *she* is. I reckon he's paid his debt to society. You gents might want to go fetch a police matron before you carry her anywhere to lock her up. For she is surely a big fibber, and you know how female suspects like to say mean things in court about the arresting officers."

So the senior copper-badge sent his junior partner to recruit some safer backup. As he joined the group around the couple at Longarm's feet, Doc Morrison said, "I'm missing something here. I can see from the way this lady is carrying on that she and the stepson you just shot were up to something wicked, and I knew Big Dick Palmer well enough to say that if I'd been wicked with his woman, I'd feel safer with him dead. But what was all that about bloodhounds out to the Lazy P and that missing bride of Little Dick's?"

Longarm said, "You can see Miss Aurora don't want to tell us where Fiona Palmer née Maguire wound up. But if I let some bloodhounds at some of Miss Fiona's underwear, they'll surely lead me to where these lying lovers buried her body under the floor tiles out yonder."

Aurora Palmer glared up at him and hissed, "You're just guessing!"

Longarm shook his head and said, "Nope. Eliminating some more. It would have been taking a mighty big risk had the two of you buried a body outside the house where you might have been seen by the hired help running free as chickens all about. It would have been risky to spare had you buried her under the tiles of anywhere but her own locked room. So that's where I figure we'll find her, and I hope you can see you are rapidly running out of secrets to confide in me, if you want to save your pretty neck for your old age, Miss Aurora."

So she suddenly began to talk, in front of three witnesses as well as Longarm. Once she'd started, she couldn't seem to stop, and by the time that other copper-badge returned with a police matron, she was starting to repeat herself.

Longarm let her go over it once more so the junior copper-badge and another woman could bear witness if need be. Then he let them carry her away. She was still trying to explain she wasn't really a bad girl, but had done it all for love.

Doc Templer said he'd see that the county coroner's crew would get the late Little Dick Palmer over to the Del Rio Morgue. So Longarm ambled on down to the Western Union to wire a full report to his boss, Marshal Vail. He knew old Billy was likely to shit when he got such a telegram at a nickel a word. But even when you left out the ands, ifs, and buts, it was a complicated tale of tangled treachery. So what the hell.

Setting the whole web of intrigue down on yellow paper with a lead pencil clarified things in his mind a mite, and this was just as well if he ever wanted to see his saddle and saddlebags again.

When he got back down to Ciudad Acuña the day after that coroner's inquest he'd had to attend, he found a mighty pissed-off La Blondita had ordered his McClellan locked away where he wasn't about to get at it unless he asked her for it polite and personal.

So as they were propped up in her four-poster, sharing a smoke as well as a sensuous siesta, La Blondita grudgingly allowed she was glad he'd shot that pest El Pico. But she was still confused about that missing redhead and that *muy grotesco* ransom some *pendejo,* if not El Pico, had demanded for her return.

Longarm passed her the cheroot and patted her bare shoulder as he told her, "You ain't been paying attention, *querida mia*. All that razzle-dazzle about a ransom deal that was fated to fall through was part of the plot to hide the simple fact that they'd murdered Fiona Palmer née Maguire at the Lazy P on her wedding night!"

La Blondita demanded, "For why? Would have been easier not to have married her if he hated her that much, no?"

Longarm said, "No. Two reasons. We got Aurora Palmer to confess she'd married Big Dick for his money, found him a dud in bed, and commenced to fiddle with a son who hated the big blowhard during her *own* honeymoon. But for all his opinionated ways, Big Dick Palmer was no total fool, and some of the help had started talking too. It ain't easy to diddle a woman down the hall from her husband in a house full of Mexican gals, no offense. So Little Dick took to courting an army brat named Fiona Maguire up to Fort Stockton. That was reason number one. Nothing much was supposed to come of such courtship. But then we get to reason number two. Poor Fiona took his courting serious. She was a pretty little thing but not too bright, and a Papist enlisted man's daughter. So she'd been used as a sort of dick-wiper by junior officers until this handsome *ranchero* came a courting, and this time she announced her engagement to her hot-tempered menfolk."

He took the cheroot back, inhaled a mellow drag, and went on to explain, "I just wired some pals in the War Department about those brothers Maguire. Don't ever get the brothers Maguire to suspecting you of abusing their kid sister. Having been told as much by his own army pals, Little Dick felt trapped and didn't know what to do, until his literally wicked stepmother proposed they kill a flock of birds with one wedding."

La Blondita brightened and said, "*Yo comprendo.* Was only for to keep others from knowing he was fucking his stepmother he married a *cabeza roja* he did not really like, no?"

Longarm said, "Yes, and then it gets dirtier. Once they had Big Dick miles from the kitchen run by his own wife, and surrounded by all sorts of friends and possible enemies, they poisoned him, hoping he'd die in Comstock so's his son and heir could console a young widow who would naturally go on living with him and his own bride at the family home."

"That sounds like a nice dirty plan," said La Blondita. "So what went wrong with it?"

Longarm said, "Everything. Big Dick didn't die, and thanks to her not being the virgin of Fort Stockton after all, Fiona demanded and got the manly attentions she thought she had coming to her, until the wicked stepmother who'd been enjoying the same favors from her groom stormed in with a rolling pin and bashed her brains in on her wedding night."

La Blondita grimaced and said, "I cannot stand jealous women. Is hard for to run a place like this when the wives find out about it. I would have allowed the *pobrecita* a little harmless fun with a lover if it meant the two of us would now be safe from a jealous husband."

Longarm shrugged his bare shoulders and replied, "The jails in both our countries would be less crowded if everybody was as sensible as you and me about harmless fun. But the hot-tempered Aurora killed her rival, finished what she'd been doing to Little Dick when she'd died, and then they buried her under the tiles of that same bedroom. So the very next morning Little Dick had to leave for this border town with his new bride, before anyone else could ask her how she'd enjoyed their wedding night. After she'd waved the happy couple off in a shay with its folding top up, Aurora excused herself to ride over to Comstock, to the west, for some shopping. Only, then she rode south to Del Rio, bought a red wig, and joined her lover in that *posada* for some more passionate slap and tickle the staff still talks about. Once they'd established memories of a honeymooning Anglo couple at the *posada,* they only had to make her disappear from that crowded market. It's easy to just walk away in a crowd. After we arrested her, Aurora Palmer confessed she'd simply hired two Mexican *vaqueros* to escort her over to the Burro Mountains and back. She told them it was to drop something off at that *posada*. They didn't care, as long as she paid them double day wages. She didn't tell them she meant to scribble that note on the wall. She simply let them loiter about, leaving a sort of sinister impression, until she signaled it was time to ride back here to Ciudad Acuña, where she got rid of that wig and the dead gal's duds she'd been wearing, and rode on home from her shipping trip to Comstock."

"*Pero no comprendo*. For how did she fool Perrita and her *sabuesos*?" La Blondita asked. Then she grinned like a mean little kid and said, "But of course. They were smelling the dead woman's sweat-stained clothing. For why did they kill the man of the house after that?"

Longarm said, "The son and heir he'd always low-rated and treated like a kid wanted to be the man of the house, and his stepmother wasn't looking forward to a big man with a flabby little organ-grinder in Little Dick's place. So they figured he might as well have a relapse so the two of them could console one another whilst the rest of us searched in vain for a bride who'd been kidnapped in Mexico or just possibly run off with a Mexican. Aurora flirted in front of folks with an innocent ranch foreman as another diversion. She sure had one sneaky mind for a gal who couldn't abide cussing at the table."

La Blondita laughed dirty and opined, "Was too bad for them her younger lover had not so much sneak on his mind. A real man would have made love to the one with red hair and the one with gray hair at the same time and—listen, is this girl downstairs who might enjoy it if I showed you what I meant, eh?"

Longarm sighed and said, "I don't know, *querida*. That Chinese gal, Miss Sinverguenza, was lots of fun, but I really ought to be thinking of heading on down the road."

La Blondita grabbed his old organ-grinder as she coyly replied, "Hey, who said anything about another *escena chingo* with the same two *muchachas*, eh? Is this *new* girl downstairs, she says she is part French and part Hungarian, but I think her *culo* looks more Polish and I would not wish for her to think I am a *lesbiana fregada*. So I was wondering if you would be willing for to help me, how you say, break her ice?"

To which Longarm could only reply, snubbing out his cheroot, "Well, I do owe you some favors and I can always head on down the road some other time."

Watch for

LONGARM AND THE MUSTANG MAIDEN

255th novel in the exciting LONGARM series
from Jove

Coming in February!